Gold Man Review

Gold Man Review is published once a year by Gold Man Publishing in Salem, Oregon.

Subscriptions available at www.goldmanpublishing.com

The editors invite submissions of previously unpublished works of fiction, nonfiction, and poetry. Manuscripts can be submitted at www.goldmanpublishing.com by following our submission guidelines.

Copyright 2014/2015 Gold Man Publishing / Gold Man Review LLC.
P.O. Box 21391
Keizer, OR 97307
Printed by Gold Man Publishing
ISSN: 2162-8238
ISBN: 978-0-692-31111-0

Contents

Letter from the Editors

This is the year of the stranger for *Gold Man Review*. Not just the people you meet but don't really know, but the moment when you realize someone you love is actually a stranger, or you are a stranger to yourself.

It's a strange new world that we find ourselves in, expanding our reach to the entire West Coast, and transitioning from a newborn literary journal to a mature publication with notables in *The Best of American Essays* anthologies.

Literature, it turns out, is the realm of strangeness. It's the place we go to see how strange we have become and what other kinds of strangeness can exist. Where language, which always seems so familiar as we use it to get through the day, untangles itself from its usual meanings, and the words of other people run through our heads in the act of reading silently to our estranged selves.

We see this in Geronimo G. Tagatac's, Patrick Mathiasen's, and Joyce Tomlinson's stories about how aging turns us all into strangers, and makes us see the world as if it too is a stranger, unknown and unknowable.

We see it again from another perspective in such pieces as Harry Demarest's and NT McQueen's stories, where the self is the strangest stranger of them all.

As you read through this year's contents, we hope you enjoy the vacation from your self and from your usual haunts. We know we did.

Thank you for reading and writing!

Sincerely,

Gold Man Review Editors

Managing Editor
Darren Howard

Editor-in-Chief
Heather Cuthbertson

Project Editor
Nicklas Roetto

Executive Editor
Marilyn Ebbs

Editor
Lois Rosen

Associate Editor
Michelle Modesto

No. 61 1952

Mark Rothko
New York 1955 as Rust and Blue
London 1961 as No. 61
Zurich 1971 as Brown, Blue, Brown on Blue
Brussels, Basel, Rome, Paris, Los Angeles

by Elizabeth McLagan

1.

Wandering surfaces brimmed and surging,
soot-oiled clouds spill a post-inferno
of heavy metals, a fog too thick. Or
just some hover and shift, a restless
river overfloating sweet sky dirt.

2.

Now, below, a spell of calm—lake wash,
robin's egg, queen of heaven blue.
White bleeds through like an answer.

3.

Here is your stubborn incantation,
this scratched momento of thoughts—
small stars descend the stars,
a few reeds sway a swamp. Blackbird
out of time—rust and blue, sings
brown—blue—brown-on-blue—

An Elegy for Alice

Who Called Out of the Blue on Her 54th Birthday
in April 2010, Said She Was "Tying Up Loose Ends" before Heading
into a Period of Major Surgeries, and Died a Brief Eighteen Months
Later of Complications from a Recurring Infection

by Nancy Flynn

There is no one behind the curtain, able to fix, eager to mend.
Even with the eggs at room temperature, sometimes you beat the whites
       and they still won't peak.

All those fields—rutabaga, tomato, turnip—that once filled
       the no man's land between
       the dike and your backyard fence,
       gone like you,
       victory gardens ceded to asphalt,
       to a trail of B.B.s, cigarette butts, beer cans,
       the ubiquitous plastic bag snagged and waving from a branch
       to two girls, motherless.
Our river's edge.

According to the moon, the day you died was the best
       for picking above-ground crops.
You, one of the ripe ones.
You, lost before the upper limb of the sun lifted above the horizon, 6:44 A.M.
A day of no rainfall or gusts, ten hours and seven minutes of light.

Georgie Steps Out

by Les Brady

All George had to do was pick up the phone, make the call. But he only stared at the leaking kitchen faucet—about a drop every twelve or fourteen seconds, he surmised—then at the phone hanging on the wall, and instead of simply lifting the receiver and punching the number he hurried out the back door, crept tentatively toward the valve, and shut off water to the whole house, just to keep the drip at bay.

Whom to call?

In the Yellow Pages plumbers abound. George knew this. But which? Some boasted specialties in drains, but this was no clog. What of those who knew not only water but heat? Was there some secret advantage? And such expense.

Of course.

Call Jeri.

"Hello-o?" Jeri answered, making a double syllable of the O. George loved the sound of her greeting, loved most everything about her—that she understood the mechanical world, the mysteries of harnessing water and heat and air; the way she looked, her cropped bleached cut, soccer-player body, unshaven pits; the sound of her voice, not feminine, not masculine, but unique, unfettered.

"It's me. George."

"Hey, George. What's up?"

"Oh, nothing. Really ..."

"*George?*"

"I mean. It's just—"

"Come on."

"It's not a big problem."

"You need help changing your oil again?"

Oh, no, he thought: *so complex. So complex...*

That was how they'd become acquainted, a conversation about automotive maintenance that had dropped from the sky so fortuitously that George did not believe it could be happening. It was the day they would fire him from the job at the construction company where he'd worked in the office, answering the phone, filing prints and mailing out proposals. But he'd found himself compelled to accomplish all these tasks at times simultaneously, and could neither justify neglecting one for another nor figure what to do with the receiver in his right hand and a permit application in his left.

His problem was not simply a lack of multitasking acumen, but a challenge that had plagued George his entire life, when from his earliest memories he could recall sitting in a kindergarten yard, hiding inside the hollow well of a large play structure while the other children sat in a circle on the grass rolling a large inflated ball randomly back and forth to fellow classmates; the actual activity of rolling the ball had not confounded George, but when he tried it previously had felt daunted by the seemingly simple decision of to whom he should roll.

Teachers eventually voiced concerns to school counselors, who in turn spoke to George's parents, who seemed not the least bit perturbed; George, they explained, had always, simply, been George, and Mom and Dad treated him and his proclivities with uncommon ease. But they relented nonetheless, allowing the various scholastic and psychological professionals to evaluate their son, all in an attempt to extract a concrete conclusion that unequivocally explained his behavior. Surely, the experts believed, he was beset by Obsessive-Compulsive Disorder, perhaps Attention Deficit/Hyperactivity Disorder, was possibly borderline Autistic; of course they'd assumed to discover at *least* a low IQ. But to their collective chagrin the experts found that settling on any of these conclusions proved mostly unfounded. Yes, George exhibited some obsessive traits—preferring his pens and pencils on opposite sides of his desk—but not much more than the average person. George did not display the impulsivity or inattention of someone with AD/HD; in fact, his behavior could be characterized as *hyper*-attentive. While George was certainly shy, he failed to display the debilitating lack of social skills and poor language development of an autistic child. And, as if in a final stroke of unwitting triumph, George scored an IQ of 163, which made him, technically, a genius.

What they did finally understand about George was that, given a singular task and the quiet concentration needed to accomplish it, he would apply all means necessary and solve the problem, thoroughly and correctly. When he grew older and progressed in school, his teachers discovered that he possessed an aptitude in mathematics—appeared to enjoy the discipline—and when given a single equation to solve did so with alacrity. But administered a test with multiple equations, George could not, no matter how explicit the directions, decide on which problem to solve first, their numbered succession a complete irrelevance.

The drawbacks beset him because of this focal singularity weren't why they fired him from the construction company, though. In fact, he was well-liked by the entire staff; when he stared at a ringing phone and back at the file in his hands, over and over, it had become almost endearing to the trades people and mechanical technicians, whose sun-hewn faces and burly demeanors could not have contrasted more widely with George's soft, slight, hesitant self; the crew only grinned and shook their heads, took the overflow calls when they could. And he would have continued to endear himself to the staff, would have remained the company's odd, flawed administrator, if he could only have found a way to arrive at work on time, some days at all.

On that brutal August afternoon with the air conditioning down and all the HVAC techs on job sites, he watched out the window as Jeri abandoned the down unit and returned to the shop interior.

"Get a couple fans going, George. This is gonna take a while."

She leaned studiously over a set of schematics, arms straight and hands planted flat and firm on the table, and George watched a rivulet of sweat seep from her underarm, lace down an auburn tendril to disappear beneath her tank top. Not much excited George, but when he watched her there the quick vision of those straight, tawny arms coaxed a sensation that made him jump and rise, hurrying to the water cooler for a cup.

"You okay, Georgie?"

"Fine." The water ached ice-cold on his teeth.

Jeri returned to the schematics and George finished his cup, peered through the slits in the Venetian blinds at the molten parking lot. Then Dave, the owner, poked his head through the open office door and asked if George could please, just for a few minutes, come on in.

Doom-ridden thoughts of being fired had often danced demonically in his mind, and he'd imagined languishing in tatters on the street, sore from sitting on the cold concrete, begging change from the knees of passersby. But when it actually happened Dave simply sighed from across the desk, even looked a little sad, said it just wasn't working out, and he'd be happy to provide a reference when George needed one. Then Dave stood and handed George an envelope, squeezed his shoulder like a friend, and said good luck.

"Whatcha got there, George?" Jeri spoke absently, one eye on the drawings. "That for me?"

Les Brady 5

"No."

George walked to the exit door, one step from the blanketing heat.

"It's for me."

It took some time, but Jeri finally convinced him to wait for her at the tavern down the block until 3:30—quitting time. George sat in the unfamiliar confines, hunched over the dark, padded edge of the bar drinking Diet Coke and gorging from a bowl of Chex Mix. He didn't remember the last time he'd eaten, not that he couldn't have made something, just that it was always such a daunting process, full of conflicting choices, avoided until he could no longer stand the acid churning in his stomach.

"I'll have a draft, Hank," Jeri belted in a burnished alto. George looked up and saw her in the back-bar mirror striding nearer, their contrasted images more than palpable to him, and as he gazed upon her reflection, rendered in such extreme proximity to his own, he felt behind his eyes the pressure and sting of pent up tears.

When he turned to his left, she was actually there.

"I talked to Dave, but ... I'm sorry, George."

"It's all right."

"How come you were late so many times?"

"My car."

"What's up?"

"It needs ... I have to ..."

"What?"

"Oil."

"Oil?"

"Yes."

"What about it?"

"It's spent. Probably burned. You explained to me once—you were very emphatic about the issues, though I fecklessly ignored them—about how viscosity breaks down, and that valves can potentially—"

"George. Are you telling me you need an oil change?"

George nodded.

"Jiffy-Lube! Twenty minutes."

"Oh, *no.*"

"How you been getting to work?"

"I walk."

"Where from?"

"West Central."

"By the Greyhound station?"

"Mm-hmm."

"That must be five miles!"

"Six."

"Oh, Georgie ..."

He watched Jeri down her beer, plant the empty mug on the bar with a resolute clunk, then turn toward him.

"Come on." She tugged his arm.

"Where?"

"To change your oil."

He'd allowed himself fantasies, of course, followed by stern self-admonishment; she was a co-worker, after all, and was now even offering the supportive assistance that could solidify friendship.

"Wow, that's an original, Georgie." Jeri leaned out the window of her pickup and gazed at the '74 Dart.

"My dad's."

"I believe it. So, where's your parents?"

"Gone."

"Oh, I'm sorry, George."

"No. I mean, gone, as in bought a new car. Packed and left for Palm Springs. Better for their health."

"Arthritis?"

"Etcetera."

"And they left you the Dart *and* the house? Sweet!"

George watched Jeri jump from the cab of her pickup and hoist a tool belt over her shoulder, then lean into the bed and with both hands extract a framelike device made of wooden two-by-eights.

"First thing's you got to make sure to center her on the ramp. Always easier to do with a buddy."

Buddy. George smiled.

Jeri directed George, who stood in front of the car and gave hand-signal adjustments while focusing intently on the rails of the homemade ramp. This process took far longer than it should have because if George determined that the wheels were off center by a fraction he'd direct Jeri to back up and begin the

Les Brady

entire approach all over again.

From under the belly of the car Jeri instructed George on the proper procedure, and while he acknowledged the sturdy sounds of "oil pan" and "drainage
bolt" and "filter wrench" with exuberant if feigned engagement, all he could see,
all his consciousness could absorb, were the ropes of Jeri's arms—the glint of
her sweat-veiled muscles—bare from the shoulders down.

Which certainly played a roll in George's ultimate choice of whom to call for
plumbing help. True, another plumber would have charged actual money, and
George had none to speak of since what little he earned he reserved for the bills
(after many utility shut-offs, he was shown finally how to set up payment inter-
vals online), the occasional Quick-Stop meal (the durable consistency of corn
dogs comforted him) and the continued indulgence in a preoccupation greater
perhaps than the one he held for Jeri.

"Always remember," Jeri began, "if you're gonna use channel-locks on
chrome, wrap a rag around the fitting so you don't scratch the finish."

George nodded intently, fully aware that he would never use such a device
on anything, the luster of its finish notwithstanding. After watching Jeri replace
the O-ring and re-tighten the aerator—and with great trepidation wait while she
opened the main water valve—George stared at the kitchen faucet.

"Go ahead, George. It's okay now."

With the assurance, he opened the cold-water side, then the hot, then both
simultaneously, shut each respectively and acknowledged from the completely
drip-free result that it was, indeed, okay. At least for a few savored seconds, for
when he finished relishing the efficacy of Jeri's repair, George turned and realized that she still stood in the middle of his kitchen and he hadn't the slightest
inkling on earth what to do.

Not that he hadn't imagined her there, she in his home, he in her life: holding the flashlight while she searched the panel for a tripped breaker; securing
the ladder with both hands when she reached the high rungs; bringing her
something cold to drink on a particularly hot day in the yard. But he was so elat-
ed when she'd agreed to help with the leaky faucet, more so when she'd actually
shown up, that George had simply neglected to think things through this far.

After a few awkward moments—George leaning wide-eyed against the counter watching Jeri smile at him—he realized two things: 1) it *was* a hot day and 2)
despite that they were not *in* the yard, nor had Jeri been *doing* yard work, and
though it was entirely possible that she did *not* indulge thusly in such things,

George determined it acceptable to offer a refreshment.

"Diet Coke?"

"Sure." Jeri smiled even wider, then added, motioning toward the chair next to the kitchen table, "May I?"

"Oh!" George exclaimed, "Of course! How could I have—"

"George?"

"Yes?"

"It's okay. But that Coke sure would taste good."

He'd succeeded in fetching the sodas, glasses filled with thick, square ice cubes (George could not abide the random shapes of bagged ice), even opened Jeri's and poured her a glass; he smiled at this particular triumph.

"What're those?" Jeri pointed at a half dozen of what appeared to be some sort of carrying cases lined next to one another at the base of the kitchen wall. George's mind raced; he'd certainly not envisioned this, but reasoned that if by some act of grace Jeri should want to share future Diet Cokes, George would sooner or later have to reveal the cases' contents. So he retrieved one and un-zipped the lid, reached inside and extracted a small intricate and colorful object, placing it on the table immediately in front of Jeri.

She squinted at the tiny figure. "Who painted him?"

"I, um ... I ..." George said, paused, then continued: "I."

He quickly pulled more figures from the case and set them in particular order on the table.

"You painted these yourself? You're shittin' me."

"Uh ... no."

"George, these are *amazing!*"

"Well ... They're miniatures."

"So, how long does it take to paint 'em?"

"That one? Forty-six ... No, wait." He ciphered a computation in the air with his finger. "Fifty-two."

"Fifty-two?"

"Hours."

George displayed for Jeri the majority of his collection, kept in a catacomb of tiny plastic enclosures fit snuggly into the pliant yet sturdy nylon carriers that looked more befitting the gear of a Special Forces commando.

"There must be dozens," Jeri said.

"Hundreds."

One-by-one, George extracted the tiny figurines, all of a warlike ilk, though either so ancient-looking or so extra-terrestrial that their appearances nearly obscured their purpose. Some stood in perpetual attention, awaiting the scrutiny of a commanding officer; others flew in eternal frozen attack, mouths forever agape, arms, legs and weapons molded in mid-motion that would never progress.

"So, you just paint 'em and put 'em away?"

"No. They're for the *game*."

"What game?"

George handed Jeri an inch-thick hardcover volume with dark glossy veneer. The cover boasted clashing minions akin to George's figurines. Jeri opened the book in the middle and scanned wide-eyed at the columns of tight paragraphs, words of too-small font, complex rules and indecipherable tables of numbers and arcane terms.

Though it may seem a contradiction, George's eccentricities and subsequent inabilities had never kept him from poring over the game's guidebooks, page after grim page, over and over, until he could recall at will every guideline of combat, every nuance of magic, all the inner workings of the dangerous fantasy world that framed the game; he'd been reading and re-reading the guide books for over two decades.

"So, this is like the rule book? Looks real hard."

George smiled a close-lipped smile and swept an open, upturned palm toward the bookshelf behind him; he watched Jeri follow his hand and gaze at the dozens of books, differing only in their ascending volume numbers emblazoned on successive spines from the tome Jeri held in her lap.

"You're telling me you need to know all those, too?"

George sighed and felt the deep, warm satisfaction that only manifested in his being when he'd completely transcended the verbal.

"I think I'll stick to looking at 'em," Jeri said.

"My latest." George reached into one of the cavernous cases and extracted an inch-high captain of the guard, stance wide and firm and holding a purple-plumed helmet in one hand and in the other a brutal halberd butted firmly into the ground. A crimson sash wrapped his tiny armored body and the white of his pinpoint eyes beamed a savage intensity.

"So, who do you play with?"

"Players at the game store. Some possess very advanced skills."

"That's cool, George. I never knew you had friends."

"Not friends." George punctuated the distinction: "*Opponents*."

"Oh."

"How is your Diet Coke?"

"Good."

"Would you like more ice? I prefer the cubes as they tend to maintain symmetry and stem the problem of melting."

"George, may I ask you a personal question?"

"Yes?" George smiled, watched Jeri avert her eyes momentarily, then return her gaze toward his own.

"Do you have any friends?"

George sat completely still, his expression unchanged. He watched the wrinkles on Jeri's face transform from a look of uneasy concern to a smooth flush of exuberance.

"Listen, I'm having a barbecue next Saturday. You'll know people. From the crew at work. And they'd love to see you. They ask about you all the time."

George's face contorted. "They fired me! They think I'm a fool!"

"No, George, no one thinks that. Dave just asked about you the other day, if you were working yet and stuff."

George envisioned the confusion of the crowd, the daunting task of interaction. How would he know what to say? Whom to speak to? When? About what? He saw himself where he always ended in a crowd: a forgotten corner, staring like a hidden observer, someone others literally passed by as if he weren't there at all. But he also saw another image: Jeri, speaking to him, smiling at him, allowing her arm to brush his.

"Well," George determined, "I *will* have to check my schedule."

All week George thought of nothing but the barbecue. He'd asked what he could bring, thought that beer would be appropriate even though he preferred Diet Coke, but Jeri had told him that an entire keg of beer would be present, and George thought this fascinating and curious since he'd never been around a keg of anything, and he wondered if it were possible to obtain a keg of Diet Coke.

He barely ate, hardly slept, slipping uncontrollably between the elation of spending time with Jeri and the anxiety of interacting with a band of mostly strangers. Friday night he went to the game store, intent on slaughter. And slaughter he did, using every tactic and evasion, luring his opponent into a final ambush that lay waste to his every minion; afterward, the teenaged kid looked at George and said, "Dude, that's fucked up," but George felt no remorse, secure in the knowledge that his adversary would spend the next week poring over

Les Brady

strategy to plot revenge.

Exhausted from battle, George slept till dawn.

Saturday morning.

The Day of the Barbecue.

He rose and showered, dressed in his best shirt and pants, then re-thought the wardrobe decision since he assumed people who went to barbecues wore shorts, maybe even sandals. But George owned neither. So, he compromised with a gaming tee shirt, but when he looked in the mirror at the blood-spattered warriors and decapitated troll he deferred to the dress shirt, rolled up the sleeves and left the collar open. He took a cold twelve-pack of Diet Coke from the fridge and grabbed his keys. The only problem being that it was now six-thirty in the morning. The barbecue would not commence for another seven and one-half hours.

He returned the twelve-pack to the fridge, then decided to *have* a Diet Coke, opened the door, plucked a can and pushed open the tab. The soda exploded like a chilled grenade, spraying George's shirt. He panicked and dropped the can, and it spun like a Chinese firework, soaking his pants.

He put on sweats and a tee shirt and drove to the Laundromat, saw that it did not open until ten, returned home and resolved to hand-wash. He poured detergent into the kitchen sink and ran water until it was sufficiently warm and the sink held a head of suds, then submerged his soiled garments and let them soak, rubbing them furiously together before rinsing. The rinsing took a very long time since he'd used far too much detergent. Then there was the problem of drying. He hung his pants and shirt over the shower curtain rod: three hours later, still soaked.

He tried the railing of his back porch, hoping that the sun and wind would do the trick, but the breeze swept both pants and shirt into an alleyway puddle. George noticed his clothes gone only after another two hours, sufficient time for automobile tires to have made their marks. Dejected, he tried another soak-and-scrub, but knew he had no time to air-dry. He turned the oven on and hung pants and shirt over the open door, returning to the kitchen table where he could both monitor the drying clothes and continue to paint.

The smoke alarm's shriek caused George to throw paintbrush and figure into the air. He leapt toward the oven, grabbed the smoking garments and threw them into the sink, running cold water full bore. And after he'd aired out the house and shut off the faucet, George realized two things: 1) that it was now two o'clock—the time that the barbecue was to begin—and 2) the drip from the kitchen faucet had returned. He concluded that it had worsened, estimating a drop every seven to nine seconds, then shook his head, wondering how he could have ruined Jeri's work.

I'll wear a GenCon tee shirt instead. It's older, but no blood ...

By two-forty-five George had finally finished ironing the tee shirt. In a stroke of ingenuity he'd cut the singed, damp pant legs from his khakis and fashioned a not unacceptable pair of shorts. But while doing so he envisioned the already crowded barbecue, the throng of strangers and former co-workers, others vying for Jeri's attention. He put the shirt on and sat back at the kitchen table, deciding to fix the marred paint on the figurine and simply let the day fade as his days always did; soon it would be six, nine, midnight, and George would still be lost in his painting, safe in his solitude.

The phone rang.

"Yes?"

"You're not gonna stand me up, are you?"

"Oh, no! I was just ... simply ... running late."

"Okay, well folks are asking for you, so come on over."

"I will."

"You sure?"

"Yes."

"See you soon."

George replaced the receiver gently on its base and smiled a close-lipped but genuine smile. He hurried to the bathroom mirror to check his appearance, returned to the fridge, extracted the twelve-pack, picked up his keys. When he opened the front door a thought occurred that could have trapped him inside for hours: *the oven.*

When he checked, he found it still radiating heat. Though he turned the oven off, there was the matter of the drip, and George decided again to shut off the main valve and wait. But when he reached for the knob to the back door the phone rang again.

"Yes?"

"George, if you don't leave right now I'm gonna come get you."

"I left the oven on."

"You baking?"

"No. Washing. And then the drip returned. And ... and ..."

George paused, because he had no idea how to explain the myriad thoughts crashing through his mind making complete sense to him, but unable to form

Les Brady

them into words. How could Jeri understand him? Why would she even want to? How on earth could someone so dynamic have the slightest inkling of attraction for someone like—

"George? Listen." Jeri spoke slowly, seriously. "I want you to come to my barbecue. And so does everyone else. But, especially me."

"Really?"

"Yes. So come on."

Again he hung up and smiled. And checked the oven once more, and the kitchen, bathroom and living room windows, and made sure the iron was off, and unplugged his electric toothbrush's base, and turned off all the light switches except for the porch light because that was for safety. When he'd slid his key into the front door lock, the way he always did to guarantee he didn't forget to secure the door but also make certain he didn't leave his keys inside, he paused, stepped back into the house and re-checked everything he'd checked already, trying desperately not to think of the crowd, the strangers ...

Jeri.

Then George grabbed his twelve-pack of Diet Coke and stepped out.

Road Trip

by Susan Blackaby

Side by side we climb into the Triumph,
folding like paper cranes to tuck into the bucket
seats, ducking under the cloth top,
a 58-horsepower pup tent.

Out of the chute from scruff to pavement,
careening at a shallow altitude, we lean into
curves and swerves from rut to chuckhole,
navigating the capillaries of the map,

a journey of escape and quest—the best
of both. Edges blur beyond the milky
plastic of the back window,
so that the only clear path lies ahead,

as far as the next turn or the next,
with no looking back, not even a backward
glance at past temptations, at consequence,
at Eurydice, changing a tire beside the road.

Riding To The Shore

by Liz Prato

Ginny stood on the counter of the diner decorated in tinfoil. She's my wife, if you want to call her that, which I do. She'd made bracelets and earrings and a fake-fancy necklace by folding and shaping tiny glinting pieces. She even made a tinfoil tiara, perched on her red wig from the chemo clinic. Ginny clasped a ketchup bottle to her chest. "I really didn't expect to win," she gushed. "It's such an honor to even be nominated. I have so many people to thank."

"Get your skinny ass down from there and get back to work," Joe said. He was standing over the flattop cooking us all some eggs. "Deb, get your honey's skinny ass down from there before she breaks a leg," he said to me.

I didn't care about getting Ginny's skinny ass down from there. She looked too damn pretty being all silly and shiny, like she used to be before she got sick. Her only customer at her only table was laughing his ass off anyway, and everyone else was home watching the Oscars. It didn't matter if you lived six-hundred miles from Hollywood. People still acted like all that business mattered.

"And really," Ginny said. "There's someone who deserves this award more than me, and that's my high school drama teacher, Mrs. Futtlebutt. Mrs. Futtlebutt, will you please join me on stage?" She extended a hand down to me with a dopey look in her eyes.

"Oh my," I said, clutching my throat. "What an honor." I grabbed the edge of the counter to steady myself, then crawled up next to Ginny's tennis shoes. The Formica was hard on my knees and my knees were hard on me, so I pushed myself the rest of the way up fast. Nobody could accuse me of being young and graceful, that was for damn sure.

Ginny handed me the ketchup bottle. "Mrs. Futtlebutt, this is for you." She placed the tinfoil tiara on my head.

"You sure are a couple of silly broads." Joe stood there holding plates of fried eggs and hash browns. "Now get down before your dinner gets cold."

We helped each other down. Ginny wiped off the counter with a rag, just like she did a dozen times a day, and we slid into a booth with Joe. I put Tabasco and ketchup on my eggs, but Ginny ate hers plain. That was about all her stomach could handle those days.

When the phone rang, Ginny got up to answer it. "Eureka Diner, Home of the World's Best Eggs, Crafted by Joe the Master Chef. How can I assist you this evening?"

"Wish she'd stop answering like that," Joe said through a mouth of hash browns. I knew he didn't really mean it—there was just no way anybody could.

Ginny screamed. Not in a scary way, but more like she was at a Beatles concert. "No, really?" she said into the phone. "When? For how long? Oh, I can't wait! I love you!"

"Got competition, Deb?" Joe elbowed me in the ribs.

"Ha, ha." There was only one other person Ginny said I love you to: her daughter.

Ginny slid back into the booth. "You'll never guess what?"

"Christy coming to visit?" I said into my runny yolks.

"Yes! Tomorrow. She's driving up first thing in the morning."

Christy used to come stay with us for a week in April and another at Christmas and for six long ones in the summer. That was before she turned eighteen, when she still had to do what the custody agreement said. Too bad that agreement said nothing about looking me in the eyes, or saying anything more than, "Let me talk to my mom," when she called, which wasn't real often. Not since Ginny got sick. Not since I was left to handle it all.

After Ginny's shift was done, we went straight home. We brushed our teeth side-by-side, taking turns spitting in the sink and passing the water cup to rinse. The sink was only a couple feet from the toilet, which was only a couple of feet from the bathtub—everything was only a couple of feet from each other—but we knew how to make it work. We'd even figured it out with Ginny kneeling in front of the toilet and no room for me behind her. I could sit in the bathtub and reach one hand over to Ginny's back to try and cool it off.

We got in bed under the wedding quilt my brother Keith gave us. Ginny curled onto her side, and I curved around her back. I put my hand on Ginny's stomach. I didn't rub, because that could be too much for her sometimes. But she liked a little pressure there. A little warmth.

"You should sleep in tomorrow," I said. Ginny didn't have to be at work until eleven—Joe was real good about letting her work short shifts.

"I might go in early," she said. "See if I can catch part of breakfast and pick up some extra tips."

Maybe it seemed like Ginny should save her energy, but it was so good when she got it that she used it right up. I didn't blame her. The energy surged in waves, and when a pretty one came along, she just had to jump on and ride it to the shore.

Ginny turned toward me, leaving a space just big enough for her to lay a hand on one of my breasts. She traced my nipple with her fingers, traced it like you run a finger through soft sand. That might have been all, just Ginny tracing my nipple, because she often wasn't up for much more, but my nipple got hard and I felt myself going warm and wet. I ran my hand from Ginny's ass up to her head. Ginny moaned when I got to her smooth scalp. It turned out there were lots of nerve endings up there, and it felt good to Ginny in a way neither of us had known about before the chemo. Even though Ginny was in remission and her hair could grow back, she kept on shaving her head and wearing that silly wig.

Ginny slid her hand off my breast and traveled down to my stomach, and when her hand was there, on my stomach, I hoped that my healthy insides would soak into Ginny's palm and make their way back inside of her. Even though some of her stomach had got cut out, I figured there was still a way for her to be whole. Her hand kept sliding down and between, and then it was less about Ginny's hand and more about her fingers.

She'd caught a pretty wave and we were going to ride it to the shore.

I once saw a movie about three girls who were maids at a resort. They'd go into a room together and talk about boys and surfing while they stripped beds and folded towels and wiped down sinks. But I worked alone at the motel, pushing my cart from room to room.

I knocked on a first-floor door. "Housekeeping," I said, even though there was probably no one to hear. Most people only slept in Eureka for one night on their way to or from the Redwoods. By the time I got to a room, the sheets were heaped and the towels were damp, the trash nothing more than a strand of dental floss or a dirty Band-Aid.

The inside of the room looked like a ghost town with pages of the *Times-Standard* scattered over the floor. A pink lipstick stain rimmed a plastic cup next to the bed. I went about changing sheets and scrubbing the toilet and vacuuming the floor. It was the kind of job you didn't need to think much about, which was good last fall. I'd been too worried that the surgery didn't get all of Ginny's tumor and that the chemo might not get the rest. Maybe a job that didn't keep me on my middle-aged feet all day would have been nice, but at least it forced me upright. Made me move.

A shiny gum wrapper in the trash made me think of Ginny standing on the counter the night before. She used to be silly like that all the time. Her husband sometimes left her in charge of the market in Fresno while he ran to the bank or a meeting. As soon as he left, Ginny'd take over the P.A. system. "Knock, knock?" she'd say to the entire store.

"Who's there?" I'd yell from the floor.

"Interrupting sheep," she'd say.

"Interrupting shee—"

"Baaaaa!"

At least once a week Ginny brought in food for the employees, Rice Krispie squares or chocolate pretzels or pumpkin-shaped cookies. She didn't mind pitching in either. Once a customer spilled a bag of rice on Aisle 6, and a kid threw up on Aisle 4. Ginny rolled a bucket and mop out to Four, and didn't complain one bit while I swept up rice two aisles away.

After work, I stopped by the diner to see if Ginny wanted anything special from the store. She had a couple of tables, so I sat at the counter with a bowl of clam chowder. There wasn't much lying around the kitchen that morning, so all I had for lunch was a hard-boiled egg, some saltines, and two slices of American cheese. I devoured the soup, not even chewing the bits of clam.

Three pencils stuck out from the curls of Ginny's red wig. The hospital had wigs people donated after their hair grew back or after they were gone. One day I came home to find Ginny lying on the couch with one hand on her belly, and this red bouffant wig on her head. "Joe's not gonna like it," I told her.

"Well, then he can just kiss my grits," Ginny said.

Turned out that Joe got a kick out of the wig, and took to calling her Flo and fake-yelling that she was a silly broad.

Ginny wiped her hands on her apron and leaned toward me. "More coffee, babe?"

I shook my head. "Anything you want from the store?" What sounded good to Ginny changed from day to day, and there were some days when nothing did.

"Vanilla ice-cream," Ginny said. "With little brown specks in it. And noodles. And peas."

I wrote it down on a piece of paper so I wouldn't forget. Anymore, it seemed if I didn't write something down, there wasn't much chance of me remembering.

"Holy shit!" Ginny said and went for the door. Standing outside the front window was Christy, wearing jeans and a bright blue UCLA t-shirt. Her hair streamed long and blond down her back like Ginny's used to.

Ginny started screaming—I could hear that from inside—and jumping up and down. She hugged Christy and it was hard to tell if Christy hugged back because Ginny had pretty much pinned her arms.

"Is that Gin's girl?" Joe asked, squinting toward the window.

"Looks like it," I said.

"She looks older."

"Don't we all." Not that Christy cared about how old I looked or felt. I was pretty sure that girl didn't care one bit how hard I'd had it, working full time and driving Ginny to the clinic, cooking and cleaning, and wondering if there'd ever be fun again.

Ginny unpinned Christy and waved, then pointed to Christy like I might have missed the whole thing otherwise. It had been quite a while since I'd seen Ginny smile so wide for so long.

I cooked up noodles for dinner, with butter and peas, and figured we'd have vanilla bean ice-cream for dessert. Christy took one bite of the noodles and said, "Kinda bland."

"Spices are next to the stove." Ginny pointed.

Christy walked to the drawer, which was only about an arm's length from the table. Before she'd tasted the noodles, I'd asked what classes she was taking, so Christy went right on about that. "Mostly, I'm knocking out core classes," she said, sprinkling on garlic salt. "But I've got this cool psych class on Theories of Cognition and Abnormal Behavior."

"That's quite a mouthful," I said.

"Cognition means the way people think about things." Christy stirred her noodles and sat back down. "And abnormal means—"

"I know what abnormal means." I'd taken a smattering of classes at Fresno Community College when I was Christy's age. Before it got to be too much, studying, working, and paying the rent.

"You still a maid at that motel?" Christy asked. She had the same blue eyes as her mom, but they sure didn't see people the same way. "It sounds gross. Cleaning other people's toilets."

"There's much harder things than that," I said. That girl had never cleaned up after anyone a day in her life. She'd certainly never had to wipe up puke or mop up diarrhea that wouldn't go away.

"It sounds fun," Ginny said. "Learning about so many different things." She hadn't touched her noodles, but I didn't know if that was about the excitement of Christy being there, or more about her stomach.

"So, what's with the wig?" Christy asked through a full mouth.

"It's kind of fun, don't you think?" Ginny pushed and primped her curls like she was Rita Hayworth fussing to go on stage. She didn't normally wear the wig at home, at the dinner table. She usually wore a hat or a scarf or nothing at all, and when she wore nothing at all I would reach over and run a hand across her smooth head.

"It's weird," Christy said. "You can do better."

"So, what are you doing here?" I asked.

"Came to see my mom."

"Why now?"

"Well, it's spring break—"

"No, why now?" I clanked down my fork. "Why now, when she's all finished with the surgery and the chemo, why are you coming to see her now, and you didn't then?"

"Deb," Ginny reached over to touch my hand, but all she got was a fist. "She was just starting college. I didn't want her to get distracted."

"That was your decision, huh?" I looked at Ginny, who was looking at her napkin trying to pretend that the hurt hadn't dug away at her. "What about Christmas break? Or Thanksgiving? Or just some long weekend."

"College is hard," Christy said. "It takes all my time."

It was the excuse Ginny had told me and herself and everyone else again and again, so you couldn't really blame Christy for falling back on it. But I wanted Christy to tell the truth. I wanted someone else to say that Ginny being sick was so terrifying you couldn't see or feel straight, that it made you want to hide away.

"You don't know one damn thing about hard," I said.

"Mom!" Christy's voice got loud and whiny. "Don't let her talk to me like that."

"Stop it," Ginny said. "Both of you stop it, stop it, stop it!" She pulled off her wig and threw it on the table between us. It sat there limp and dull, like a circus balloon that lost all its air.

I pushed my chair back and rose up tall. I picked up Ginny's wig from the kitchen table and took it with me out the front door.

I walked for a long time. My legs and feet were already tired from pushing my cart from room to room all day, but there wasn't much else to do. I'd left the apartment without grabbing the car keys or my wallet, like some teenage drama queen. I didn't even grab a coat.

My head and hands were cold. I wanted to blame it on the moon, which couldn't even bother to get half-full. The cold light made the sequoias look like Halloween decorations, blackened cutouts from giant pieces of cardboard. I slipped Ginny's wig over my head. It was a tight fit and I had to yank it down hard.

After Ginny left Christy's dad, the last thing on her mind was being a wife again. She was plenty happy just to be making a home with me. But when they started marrying folks down in San Francisco a few years back, it just seemed like the thing to do. My brother, Keith, even said he'd come up from Fresno with a minister friend who'd do the ceremony for free.

We drove to San Francisco early in the morning and stood in line for nearly five hours. Everyone was laughing and holding hands, sharing coffee and muffins, and someone we didn't even know handed a single red rose to every couple in line. After we got our license, we took the trolley down to Fisherman's Wharf and had a glass of wine. We sat staring out at Alcatraz, wondering why someone would build something so ugly in the middle of so much pretty. When Ginny asked the waiter, he said, "They wanted the prisoners to see what they were missing." I knew they were criminals, but it still seemed cruel, forcing them to look right at what they couldn't have every single day.

By the time Keith got to us, it was all over. He'd heard on the radio. No more marriage licenses were being given out, and the ones already out there didn't count. Keith said that didn't matter none, we should still do the ceremony. His minister friend blessed Ginny and me while we kissed and exchanged rings. The fog had come on in, and we couldn't see past the bridge. Only the tops peaked through, and they didn't look golden so much as a ragged red.

I drove us home the next day, playing the radio to cut the quiet. The signal turned fuzzy about a mile into the Humbolt Redwoods. The giants made it dark like dusk in there, even though it was just past lunch. I looked over at Ginny to ask for a CD, but her eyes were closed. Her forehead rested against the window and her blond hair curled around her neck. Even in the daytime dusk, I could see the collar of Ginny's pink shirt was blotched by tears.

The red wig made my head hot and my scalp itch. I shifted it around, shoving strands of hair underneath, then pulling them back out. But there was no way to make it comfortable, so I took it off. I took off that wig and dropped it to the ground, and I stepped on it once or twice. Hard.

When I got home, the living room was hot and bright. Christy was on the couch watching TV. "Where's your mom?" I asked

"Gee, I don't know." Christy didn't move her eyes. "Maybe she's in the screening room or the conservatory or something." The girl had no intention of going for sorry, and I suppose I didn't either.

I pushed open the bedroom door. Ginny was lying on her side with a pillow scrunched underneath her. I unbuttoned my shirt and unhooked my bra, and while I was taking off my jeans, Ginny turned and watched. The sliver of moon peaking in the window made me feel flabby and ghost white. I pulled on Keith's flannel shirt, the one I'd been sleeping in since stealing it from him years ago. It was worn and ratty, but sure didn't feel that way.

"Where's my wig?" Ginny asked.

I got under the quilt, looked at the popcorn ceiling. The peaks and valleys looked like the far-away surface of the moon. "I lost it."

"What do you mean, you lost it?"

"I guess I dropped it," I said. "Out in the woods."

"How could you drop it?" Ginny sounded exhausted more than mad. "I need it. I wear it every day."

"Not every day."

There was as much room between us as could be in our double bed. I'd hate to see how we looked, like two sides of a log split by a dull axe.

"You were too hard on her," Ginny said.

"She doesn't respect me," I said. "Us."

Ginny turned to face me and the lack of light didn't matter. I could see her blue eyes just fine, her sharp cheekbones, her thin lips, bare skull. "She thinks you're why I left her dad."

"That makes no sense." I could see how Christy thought that when her folks split up because that was how young people think. But now she was in college, thinking for herself. She should have figured out it was more complicated. That a big piece of Ginny had already left him, long before I came along. That all of her was never really with him in the first place.

"She's the only family I've got," Ginny said. She had no brothers or sisters, and ten years had gone since her parents last talked to her. Ten years since Ginny decided she couldn't stay married to Christy's dad.

I reached across the small space between us. I slid my hand over Ginny's bare head. There was no wave between us that night, but no riptide either. There was just water creeping on the shore, and then draining back, leaving a

Liz Prato

blanket of smooth, wet sand.

The next day when I got home from work, Ginny and Christy weren't in front of the TV. They weren't in the kitchen, so I headed to the bedroom. I heard Christy before seeing her, heard her small, clipped whining sounds. She was on the ground next to the closed bathroom door, hands wrapped around her raised knees. Ginny was behind the door, retching up nothing but bitter bile. It used to be the tumor that made Ginny sick. Then it was the chemo. Anymore, it was because her stomach was so small it didn't empty out right. Her body knew purging would rid her of the pain.

Christy looked up at me, eyes puffy and pink. "She won't come out and won't let me in."

I crouched down next to her, the muscles around my knees straining like old rubber bands. "How long's she been in there?"

Christy wiped her nose with the back of her hand, her fist coming back wet and shiny. "I don't know. Like, half an hour, maybe."

I was still wearing my work uniform, brown polyester pants and a navy blue smock. I swiped the corner of the smock across Christy's nose. She was just a scared kid who didn't know how to deal with a sick mom. She shouldn't have to.

I reached above the doorframe for the allen key. "It's just me, babe," I said to Ginny as I let myself in.

Her body was a limp paisley on the cool bathroom floor, her ear pressed down like an Indian listening for footsteps. "Close the door."

I pushed it most of the way closed but didn't let it latch, didn't let it lock. Left some room for Christy to hear, to talk, to move. I stepped into the tub and sat with my legs long. I reached my hand out to Ginny's back, to her green t-shirt damp with sweat.

"Someone left a brochure in one of the rooms," I said. "For Lake Shasta." Nobody ever left clues of where they were going, but sometimes I could piece together where they'd been. "Prettiest picture you'd ever seen, the water like a mirror. Same color as the sky."

"Was the mountain in it?" Ginny asked

"Oh, sure." I reached over and flushed the toilet, sucking away layers of bile. "The snow was so bright that it looked like it was covered in diamonds."

The bathroom door pushed open real quiet. Christy's voice had a shakiness that didn't match up with the girl from the kitchen table last night. "You okay, Mom?"

"Been better, been worse," Ginny said.

Christy couldn't get to her mom because there was no space to crouch into. It would have been easy for her to leave, to just close the door and let us be.

"Here." I folded my knees to my chest and scooted to the other end of the tub. Christy climbed in next to me. I lifted my hand off Ginny's sweat-stained shirt and nodded there, to the damp imprint of my palm on her back.

Christy reached toward Ginny real slow, like she was moving toward a fire. Her hand landed on my palm-mark. It seemed like Christy might jerk back, away. It was easy to get scared like that, like your hand might just make the pain worse. Like it might make the disease come back. Like it might be your fault in the first place. All that fear never really went away. It just kept shifting around, trying to figure out what else to be. But Christy kept her hand steady. Her mother's back. Next to me.

I kneeled in the hard tub. I ran my hand over the landscape of Ginny's skull, over hills and rivers and flat sand beaches.

"This summer," I said, "We'll go over to Shasta. We'll get a room that looks out on the mountain." I got a discount at other motels in the chain and, maybe, if we started saving right away, there'd be enough for a couple of nights. "We'll rent a little boat and pack a picnic, and I'll row you out to the middle of the lake."

We'd have wine and vanilla bean ice-cream, if that was what Ginny wanted that day. The two of us would lie back in the sun, letting our skin grow warm and wet in the middle of the lake.

"We'll take lots of pictures," I said. "Make one into a Christmas card."

"I'll put it up on my mirror," Christy said. "In my dorm."

I couldn't see it, Christy's dorm or her mirror or the Christmas card held on by clear tape. But I had no problems seeing Ginny lying in a boat caressed by the sun, the water like a mirror, and Mount Shasta glittering nearby.

Liz Prato

On the Evening before Homecoming Parade, my Dog and I Visit Odysseus and his Wife

— for Everett Marvel, age ninety-one, Dufur, Oregon

by Penelope Scambly Schott

Tomorrow he will be the Grand Marshall of the parade.
He will wear his black suit and medals, his Bronze Star.

She stood up to hunt in the pantry for a box of dog treats
because her clever husband couldn't locate a brown box.

My much-indulged dog kept clicking her nails and sniffing
for their cat under couches and tables with fabric skirts.

He poured a huge glass of red wine from a box and set it
on a tv table in front of my chair. I raised my wine glass

to the Grand Marshall, the country boy who volunteered to
drive a tractor across no man's land to deliver the big gun

that won the battle on one Pacific island. He calls himself
a stupid farmer. The dog gave up and sat for her biscuits

and then we left them to eat their dinner in peace, walking
home past the school where now a guy with a mike mid-

football field is cranking out ... *at the twilight's last gleaming* ...
I sing in the street. Coin toss: our team chooses to receive.

A pink sunset is fading behind the newly white mountain.
Soon, beyond the lighted field, so many ancient stars.

Bridalplasty

by Jay Duret

In the course of researching reality TV for a novel I was writing, I stumbled upon a reference to a show that had previously escaped my attention. In this program, young women competed to win a "celebrity-style, dream wedding." While I found it disappointing that some people see a *celebrity-style, dream wedding* as an ultimate prize in life, that wasn't new news and I would not have paid the show any attention but for the show's name: *Bridalplasty*. What kind of a name is that? *Bridal*, fine, but *plasty*? What the hell is that?

I decided to do a little research. Turned out that *Bridalplasty* was an actual thing, a real reality TV contest that enjoyed a real life two-month run on E! Entertainment at the end of 2010. Twelve young women—all engaged or already married—competed, not just for a celebrity-style, dream wedding, but also to obtain their personal wishlist of *surgical procedures*. The winner would be entitled to all those cosmetic surgeries that make the difference between an ordinary life and, well, a celebrity-style, dream life.

Along the way to the dream wedding, there were 10 contests among the brides-to-be. To create additional tension each week, the winner of each stage was entitled to pick a surgical selection from their wishlist and have it performed by the show's resident doctor: a plastic surgeon who was, in real life, a plastic surgeon to *celebrities*. Thus, in the second week of the contest, Cheyenne received a rhinoplasty. The following week saw the Top Bride, Kristen, experience the full joy of breast implants. The surgical largess obtained by successful contestants en route to the finale included liposuction, tooth veneers, and a procedure to remove that flabby dangling fat on the underside of the upper arms. In fact, at the conclusion of one particularly joyous episode, all the brides who completed that day's challenge received coveted Botox injections.

The weekly chance to win surgical procedures did not provide the only drama. Each week a bride, the Bottom Bride as it were, was eliminated from the show amidst much weeping and remonstration. As the field shrank and the surgeries multiplied (the brides competed with noses hidden by surgical tape, I swear to God), the stage was set for the final episode.

That episode pitted Allyson; a heavyset 32-year-old blonde from Crestwood, Illinois, against Jenessa, a skinny, sharp-elbowed hustler from Wayne, New

Jersey, who had earned a reputation for her feral scheming and maneuvering. Jenessa might have been devious, but she won my heart when she pointed out that Allyson might play the victim but "after she got the lipo she went back in the kitchen and ate *hot pockets* every night." That was a good line.

Jenessa received a disappointing surprise when the judging panel for the final contest was revealed: it was the very brides who had been eliminated. With those judges, Jenessa didn't have a chance. They didn't even finish polling the judges before it was clear that Jenessa was going home without all the surgical procedures for which she yearned. But if the drama of a close vote was denied to us, we were treated to one splendid moment when Alexandra White of Atlanta, Georgia rendered the vote that put Allyson over the top. Alexandra had been given a chance to address the finalist and personally deliver her RSVP. Alexandra used her time in the spotlight to give Jenessa a nugget of ancient wisdom: "Karma is a bitch and so are you."

I could not resist doing a little research on Alexandra. I was quickly rewarded to learn that Alexandra had previously been a contestant on the *Biggest Loser* reality television program. She had not won *Biggest Loser*, and indeed her girth during *Bridalplasty* suggested that she liked hot pockets too, but she had scored a bigger prize: it had been on that program that she had met and become engaged to her fiancé. And so in that perfect karmic confluence that favors television shows devoted to the pursuit of deep meaning, Alexandra was competing on *Bridalplasty* to become the Perfect Bride for the very hubs with whom she shared the limelight on *Biggest Loser*. How big was that? What a moment.

The dramatic *piece de resistance* of *Bridalplasty* was a brilliant and carefully wrought plot device: once the contest began, the fiancé did not actually see the winning bride until after her surgical wish list had been completely fulfilled. This paved the way for one of those magic television moments, a moment so profound that the full possibilities of the medium will never again be doubted, the moment when Allyson was revealed to her fiancé in her new and improved format. Allyson 2.0.

The big reveal, the magic moment, occurred during—yes, you guessed it—their very own celebrity style, dream wedding. Picture this scene: Allyson in front of the preacher, her soon-to-be husband facing her. She was swaddled in veils and lace, utterly hidden from the eyes of her wedding party and the dozens of guests in attendance. No one could tell who she had become until the final instant before the vows when the veil was lifted and Allyson, radiant goddess, was revealed to the *oohs* and *ohmygods* and *yougottabekiddings* from the wedding crowd that included the very brides who she had bested along the way. Allyson. With the glam complexion and the golden hair, with a smile as white as the ceramic of a new toilet; Allyson with the cute nose and so many improvements that I cannot even list them here, all revealed to her lucky fiancé in that one unforgettable instant. Boom!

One might be sad that *Bridalplasty* lasted only that one incredible season, but that magical final episode will live on forever on YouTube, an enduring reminder that no matter how outrageous a situation a writer may create in a novel, real life will go one step lower.

Scarecrow's Last Winter

by Faith Allington

Last summer
you plowed and tugged
at the earth's curved bow,
sowed seeds and took stock
of the hedges,
prepared the hearths
for the long white months.

Today, at last,
you will take the pale gold
of new straw, heady
with the earth's wisdom.
Though it is winter
there is enough to spare.

Out on the ice blank fields
dry and plait the straw
under the crow's watchful eye,
treat it as reverently
as Saint Brigid, who healed the lepers
begging for food.

When I think of you now
I remember the story of Lleu
making a bride from flowers—
do you remember that tale?

It ended badly because
you can't make a human heart
out of petals
and expect it to feel
what the blood feels.

Worried Man Blues

by Amy Miller

Halfway through the song,
the dog bumped
his big black
pit bull head
against my leg
and I stopped—
small rest
between the banjo
and the guitar player
who never sits down.
My ragged chords caught
their breath, the bow
dropped and turned
and pressed against the fiddle,
freeing one hand
to hold that warm,
soft ear
with its own dark valley
of music.

Lower Lights

by NT McQueen

Since he was twelve, Homer Bagby never worked the same job for more than six months. His vocations shifted from a diaspora of miscellany and, each year, he lost a part of himself with the work. In his early twenties, he lost the tip of his left pinky finger to a skillsaw while working for Bauchmann Construction but he could not find the missing flesh and bone among the wood scraps and sawdust. Doctor Robert Jamison, during his residency, dressed the wound, and it was Homer who coined the moniker "Doc Rob." Five years later, while trimming hedges with Gabriel Jimenez, young Baldomero's mower caught a small rock and slung the stone as if from a sling and crashed into Homer's mouth, shattering his left incisor. The gaping hole in his smile always bothered Baldomero, the remainder of Homer's time with them, and they seldom spoke.

He lived in the same two-bedroom home for the last thirty-two years, nestled in a small neighborhood above the hills. Despite fate's malicious intent, he always bore a smile, even after his tooth cracked and his neighbors joked and laughed when they spoke with him. His transiency of work never interfered with his financial obligations and allowed him surplus money to purchase things he believed he needed. On the occasion he acquired a well-paying job, he saved the money in a tube-sock, rolled tight and wedged at the back of his dresser and allotted an allowance for good times. He often complained to his coworkers of the corruption of bankers and how those greedy sons-o-bitches stuck their sticky, greedy hands in everybody's pie and charged you with fees like you parked in a goddamn crippled parking space. The corners of his eyes creased and puckered along with his voice. The others often chuckled and coaxed his rants and, even as a young man, those his own age viewed him as a codger.

From the first moment he worked, Homer Bagby adopted the schema that he deserved some luxuries in his life. He never absconded his frugality yet it fueled his need for bargains. His hours apart from work included thrift-store hunting and scouring the classifieds. On the occasion he did not work during the weekends, his Saturdays and Sundays consisted of early morning garage sales, flea markets, and occasional antique shops. With each sale or store or market, he never left without a grasp on something. The bed of his Ford Ranger rarely was not filled. The scant nature of his purchases caused little alarm among his parents and sister. When they visited Homer from Fresno, they attributed the clutter to his lax attitude and encouraged him to keep things clean in case he invited a lady-friend over. Homer laughed his infectious laugh and waved a dismissive hand, changing the focus to their families and endeavors. The next visit, his father noticed the second bedroom's door closed and turned the knob in a trepid ease. The door opened a slat and, with his bulky shoulder, pressed forward and a hideous scrape followed the door open. When Homer heard the noise, a tragic reality pierced him and he shot from the kitchen table. His father stood in the doorway and Homer almost wept at the horror of that face. He closed the door and, though no one spoke of the room and conversation continued, a great unease imbued the atmosphere of his home.

The following summer, the family arrived, his sister cradling his two-month-old niece and his parents were electric with pride. But he saw the tension in his father's shoulders as he glanced obsessively toward the hallway and Homer's desperate attempts to rein those suspicious pupils caused a reunion of what he feared. When his father rose to use the toilet, Homer gripped the edge of his comfy chair and released a nervous stuttering unrelated to the conversation. When his father did not return soon, he stood, interrupting his brother-in-law's story about a routine moment of fatherhood. Around the corner, his father did not stand at the second bedroom but at the master and Homer witnessed a bitter nostalgia of that grotesque face. His father stood reticent while Homer entered the room, shuffling armfuls of cups, sweaters, stuffed animals, action figures, and vinyls still in their plastic sleeves. He told his father he just didn't have time to clean up and shoved the sundry items into the metal shelves that bordered his walls, loose items falling for they had no place of their own. His father asked him why and Homer froze with a pile of Scorpions, Twisted Sister, and Skid Row tour shirts draped over his hugging arms. He opened his mouth but could not speak.

He got a job working with Larry Holiday Jr. for two weeks at the Tower Mart by the Chalet Motel while Larry Sr. recovered. His hair had begun to thin in his late thirties so he wore a black, stained Raiders cap he found at the Hospice. He enjoyed working with Larry and they often joked with one another about the frequent customers who, as Homer described, as having a hell of a lot of problems. He was amused by the jittery nature of Oney and, once, shouted "bang" which caused Oney to duck and turn, eyes black and wild. When Mouthy Mary came in bruised, he waited till she had purchased her things and then made vile, invidious comments no man ought to hear. Larry merely offered a forced smile and Homer hated himself for what had come from him and he cursed Larry's youth.

NJ McQueen

But this position lasted only two weeks for Homer and he left the Tower Mart to work for Vlado Brinkerhoff at Winkie's Lounge washing glasses and steins and cutlery. His last day at the Tower Mart was Wednesday. He saw the bus pull up outside and slipped a dime roll from the register. Larry sorted inventory in back when he heard the fake then real gun shot and Homer's lamentable shriek. By the time Larry Holiday Jr. had emerged through the door, he caught the back of Oney's camouflaged body and Homer clutching at his eye. Blood seeped from between his fingers and he vomited curses over and over. At Doc Rob's office, he stitched up Homer's eye but, after some tests, informed him the shrapnel from the shattered glass had embedded in his eye. Homer wore an eye patch for two weeks and growled like a pirate before laughing that deep, bellow. But when the patch was removed, Homer only saw the shadow of the world from that eye.

Once, he landed a county job with sanitation and rode the back of dump-trucks, lifting bins of refuse into the back of the truck. Witnessing what others discarded fascinated Homer. When he would encounter those on his route, he mentioned items they had discarded during the week, some of more intimate matters. Once, he asked Jessica Keel about a pregnancy test while shopping with her mother for prom dresses. Another revealed letters from an affair of the late Jaspar Jerusalem. With the extra money, he bought more tube socks and increased his visits to the usual haunts. He found a faded recliner and a ping-pong table for thirty dollars each and bought them without hesitation. When he quit the sanitation job after a yard waste bin slipped from the claws and crushed his shoulder six months later, he lost himself for several months. His chest tightened in sporadic tensions without prompting and, to assuage the discomfort, his diligence to yard sales evolved to a dedication one makes to their craft. He set his alarm for four in the morning every Saturday and ravaged the forgotten treasures labeled and spread across rickety tables and dumped in bins and crates. A voracious compulsion to obtain deals fueled his hands. When he stopped for gas at the Chevron on Main Street and Halpern, an elderly man in overalls inquired how much he charged for a dump haul. Homer laughed off the misunderstanding but the residue of that reality clung to him the ride home. By the time he received the stock job at K-Mart several months later, he had lost his home to his compulsion. He slept on mounds of leather jackets, beanies, and motorcycle gloves he collected but had no place to rest and they cumulated upon his mattress. The constancy of this arrangement resulted in a lumpiness of his muscles more disheveled than the mattress he slept upon. A rancidity seeped from the clutter, a bitter stench of death and decay and he feared rats had infested his home. He promptly bought some traps with his employee discount, smiling as he claimed they were for his sister, and placed them throughout his home.

He could not find his phone, even when it rang. The possessions devoured the pragmatism of his life and he lived in a cluttered surrealism where he slunk and squeezed through a labyrinth of his own volition. Car magazines and newspapers stacked from floor to ceiling. A mannequin without arms stood sentry by the front door. He received an invitation for his niece's sixth birthday and he stared at the picture on the card, unable to accept if the child he saw was actually his blood. He rummaged through his home for old photos of his parents and sister and niece but he could not find those faces anywhere. The objects loomed around him, an insurmountable horde that welled a helplessness he could neither combat nor accept.

His lithe frame dwindled and his coworkers noticed. The outline of his molars shaped against the skin of his cheeks. Muscle wrapped around his bones so gaunt, others feared he may vanish. The deterioration manifested in his weakness and he breaked often during his shifts. While stacking cans of Pringles along the shelves, Niles Biffles, who smelled of smoke and mint, asked Homer if he ever loved anyone. He paused while placing a can on the shelf and felt tears form in the corners of his eyes. He wiped them quickly before Niles noticed and chuckled, making an obscene sexual remark about a girl he had dated in high school. Their laugh caromed within the aisle and the jovial face of the man on the Pringles cans seemed amused. From the corner of his eye, he saw a shadow. The rotund waddle of Jerome Peppers advanced, his brown eyes glancing from side-to-side as if his intentions were not known. He stopped before them and made notice that the Pringles Homer had lined on the shelves concealed that smiling face. Homer stood with his arms crossed as Jerome lectured him that he may need more training on how to properly stack shelves and other ramblings. Homer felt his cheek muscles ache and sweat gather between his palm and his forearms until Jerome's finger prodded into Homer's bony chest. As if a push of a button, Homer dropped his hands to his side and the words big goddamn nigger caromed where laughter once echoed. The blow shook him and warmth flooded his mouth as his vision seemed to absorb the fluorescent lights. The blurry shadows of Niles and Jerome wrestled into focus and, when he spoke, blood gushed over his lips and down his chin.

The bleeding stopped in the break room but the bulbous swelling constricted his speech. A great weight filled his chest and, before the paramedics arrived, he threw his red vest in the trash bin as he left. He drove to the thrift store just six blocks past Dave's Auto Repair and parked with the engine running and stared at the entrance and repeated to himself to not go in, not go in, don't go in. His mind tumbled over the possibility of that one find to end all searches and he placed his hand on the door handle. His tongue ached. As he walked through the doors and heard the greeting by the white-haired women behind the counter, the tension lifted yet he felt the horde cheer, distant and triumphant like a horrid echo of his life.

The most recent purchases had spilled from his home and he stacked them along the driveway and on his small porch. Every other day, the sunlight from his living room window lessened and he could no longer see over the pile outside, nor inside. A small shaft of light illuminated the immediate sheetrock of his ceiling near the window and cast shadows from the texture, gruesome faces all agape in some rapacious howl. The neighbors who sat in faded lawn chairs and drank cans of Tecate whispered and sneered at the degeneracy of his residence, often times tossing empty, half-crinkled cans among the clutter. When he found the cans, Homer often cursed at their shadows and stuffed the debris into his recycle bin. Then engaged in the idiosyncrasies of starting his truck until the engine coughed and vomited the build-up from its metallic lungs.

His bed was not his own and the reality of night burdened him. He saved himself one recliner as his resting place and kept a lamp based with a bronze Buddha by its side that sat precarious atop two volumes of a 1987 Encyclopedia Britannica. At night, he sat under that lamp and cuddled close to the glow, ears open to the groans and creaks around him. His head darted as phantoms strolled in his peripherals. He forced his eyes closed, only to heighten the voice of his creation around him. Beckoning. Singing. Hunger nagged at him but he dared not enter the kitchen. He carried with him the possibility of vanishing should he venture deep into his creation. Devoured. Lost. Forgotten. His eyes sought the familiar faces of his family. They came as fleeting glances desperate and pleading. Their voices called out from behind buried frames. But the papers. Records. Torn paintings. Coat racks and bags consumed those faces. He trembled between the walls. He struggled for breath. He cried out but the horde sucked the plea from the air.

He awoke to the scant sunlight and rose, his sock-clad feet crunching aluminum foil and chipped mugs. But, when he stood, a delirium pervaded his senses and he knew not which way to turn. He attempted the usual routes but they led to a door. A mound. A pile. He wondered if a fisherman felt such panic when he searched around him. Only to see the emptiness of water. Time lost its role. Material hands clawed toward him. He brushed the piles. Avalanches swept at his feet. To his shins. A collision against wood or metal or plaster. Lamps tipped across his path. New paths forged only to old. A terror tautological. Something scurried. Right there. He knew. Words. Formed. In the contours of his bedlam. Choked air. Stolen from his lungs. He saw the cabinets and the cataclysmic guards. A shrill cry from his lips he knew none could hear. The urgency of death seeped into his bones, saturated past marrow to soul. Smoke burned his eyes and he entertained the thought of hell and if the pits were cluttered and if he had created a gateway to the lake of fire. A desperate violence lashed from his hands and he pulled and ripped and tore, toppled the frenetic tongues from their towers and laughed at the Elysium of destruction. A Little League trophy he never earned tottered and reeled against his skull and he saw such wondrous colors and nostalgia buried within the horde of his mind. The familial voices so tangible and close he called for his mother and father and the niece whose face he could not recognize aloud but his speech severed by his own tongue. A shattering at his feet as his socked foot rested in an empty fish tank. His hands still clamored and the sting of smoke imbued his nostrils until he felt the curvy waist of a cold woman bearing no arms. He recoiled at her cold touch, hands frantic for the knob. Warmth tickled his ears, plugging the sound. The door swung open and he shielded his eyes. His foot caught a box and his knees clashed with the concrete and he wallowed like a dog before he crawled onto his dead lawn.

He inhaled as if it were his first breath and watched the sweet, curling smoke rise above. The crackle of consuming brush raised his head and he saw the mouth of flame devour the brush around him. He lifted himself to his feet and staggered back to the road, stumbling across potholes. Behind his home, the hills raised their fiery hands like some baleful congregation. Fiery sirens wailed around him and the neighbors watched with eyes uplifted at the force ever inching toward them, Tecate in hand. He raised his hand to his ear and fished out the pool gathered there. His life's work remained in the dereliction of his home and he spied one of the hoses coiled by the Ranger. He jogged over and grabbed the metal grooves at the end of the hose but froze with his hand on the valve. He kept his eyes on the new army descending the hill and tears squeaked from the corners of his eyes. Among the mounds of things, Homer Bagby grabbed a foldable camping chair from his driveway and sat. The fiery hands of the hill arrived. First catching the roof and spreading from shingle to shingle in a caustic dance. All that existed inside cried out in choral hisses and crackles and pops and he

NJ McQueen

moved his finger as if conducting a symphony. A grizzled neighbor walked up and tapped Homer on the shoulder. Homer turned, eyes red, and the neighbor nodded with a hand outstretched. Homer took the cold can, cracked the top, and nodded in return. He drank as the refining fire devoured his home and all it contained. The sting burned relief on his tongue and he smiled and sang an old hymn his grandmother sang when she would bathe him as a boy. He watched his life burn away and, when the roof collapsed, he clapped his hands until the ashes of his Babel reigned down upon him singing in his broken tongue, *Let the lower lights be burning send a gleam across the waves, eager eyes are watching, longing, for the lights along the shore ...*

Abandonment

by Penelope Scambly Schott

On a dry ridge above the Columbia River,
a yellow lab – the kind of gentle old dog
where when you look at his folded ears
you want to say *aw* – sprawls in the shade
of a cottonwood. The firewood is chopped
unevenly and the house needs paint. Far, far
below, on the distant bridge, if there are cars,
they're invisible, and the round eastern hills
are brown. Meanwhile, here up on the ridge,
someone came and arranged flower baskets,
tables, benches, and two scrap-iron globes,
and then that person seems to have vanished,
leaving these big gray rocks to sleep in rows
like obedient children at nap time. Nobody
is coming, and nobody is going. What if this
were the first moment after the Apocalypse,
and nothing remained but the dog and me
and that double barge just now passing under
the bridge, and the long white wake foaming
behind it?

One Big Coffin

by Harry Demarest

One big coffin. Four little coffins. And one man crying. Sobbing. Howling like I'd never heard before, and only once since. That was the time I did it myself.

The five coffins were in the back of the small chapel at the O'Mara and Marcelliano Funeral Home in Brooklyn. The man howling was Michael Doyle, my across-the-hall neighbor, sitting alone in the small alcove reserved for family. In the main chapel, there were about a dozen of us. The only one I recognized was the president of the Transit Authority. This must have been his seventh funeral since the northbound AC express had collided with the C local southbound.

I hardly knew Michael. We'd said "Hi" in the hallway a couple of times. That, and every weekday morning at 6:45, I heard his apartment door open, heard them smooch, heard her say "love you," and heard him say "I love you." When he came home at 5:30, same thing, but also the kids meeting him at the door. "Daddy, Daddy." "Play with me Daddy." "Daddy! Look at this." "Daaa-Daaa."

I never get out much since I got back from 'Nam, but I figured I ought to go to this funeral. I sat there in the fifth row and listened to the howling. There must have been music, there must have been speaking. All I remember is the howling. I don't think I could stand that much grief; not again, not after what happened in 'Nam. If it had been me, I'd've been wishing that I'd been on that C train with them.

The funeral was over soon enough and I walked over to Michael, who was bent over and still howling. I said something. Didn't matter what, he didn't hear me. I stuck around. Drove Michael home. He stopped howling a little before we got to the apartment, and pulled out a handkerchief.

In the days that followed, I heard Michael's door open and close every morning and evening, same as before. I missed the sound of his wife and kids. Michael must have really missed them. I imagined him sitting alone in his apartment, hour after hour, day after day.

I decided what the hell, I'd invite him over for pizza. The next Friday, I gave him five minutes after I heard his door open and shut. Then I went over and knocked. He didn't answer. Banged for five minutes. Still no answer. Waited a half hour and tried again. And again, no answer. I figured he was too depressed to even open the door, but I wasn't going to give up.

The next Friday, I bought a pizza and stood in my doorway starting at 5:20. When he came down the hall at 5:35, I gently took his arm while I blocked the hallway and led him into my apartment. I sat him down and we ate the pizza. I talked a bit, but he was silent, not even an uh-huh. After a while, I turned the TV on and pretended to watch sports. Michael wasn't paying attention, just moping, and yet he stayed until nine, when I got up and led him out the door to his place.

I did the same thing the next Friday, and the next, talking in as reasonable a monologue as I could. After a month of that, Michael started talking a bit. I'd talk about baseball or politics, and he'd say uh-uh and uh-huh. We made it a regular thing and every week he became a bit more conversational.

When the weather was nice, we'd open the sliding glass door to the balcony and sit out there looking down at the traffic six stories below on Bedford Avenue.

Over the course of several months, Michael told me a few things about himself. He drove heavy equipment in the Brooklyn Navy yard. Parents both dead, no family, just like me. He never mentioned his dead wife or kids, so I didn't either. We were able to have a real conversation about sports. He loved Detroit, hated the Yankees. I loved the Yankees, but didn't tell him that.

One night after about six months of Friday pizzas, he came in the door smiling. "They're letting Mikey out of the hospital next week."

Mikey, his only son. One of the four little coffins. Four years old. Fortunately, I was looking away, and he couldn't see my expression. I had to say something. "Oh … that's great," was the best I could come up with. Michael was crazy, but I sure wasn't going to be the one to tell him. And I sure didn't want them to put him in the nut house. He'd figure it out when he was ready.

The next Friday, Michael knocked on the door. "Can't come tonight, gotta take care of Mikey. Next week he should be stronger, I'll bring him."

"Great," I said, wondering just how crazy Michael was.

The whole next week I spent wondering what was going to happen. The paper had listed Mikey as dead. There'd been four coffins. There'd been no recent kidnappings and I didn't think he'd grab a kid, but you never know. Friday at the usual 5:35, Michael knocked and I opened the door. Michael walked in. Alone. "Mikey, this is my friend, Harry."

I played along. "Uh, hi Mikey."

After pizza, Michael and I sat out on the balcony and chatted. Michael kept

Harry Demarest

glancing back through the door, making sure Mikey was having fun watching cartoons on the TV. "I don't know what I'd do without Mikey," he said. "If they'd all been gone, I don't think I could've stood it. For a while, I wasn't sure he'd pull through. But here he is, good as ever. Sharp as a tack."

"Uh huh," I said. "Sharp as a tack." But I was thinking *Michael is crazy as a coot.*

After that, Michael got home ten minutes later than the usual 5:35. Picking Mikey up from childcare, he said. The Friday night pizzas went on for over a year. By then I figured Michael knew on some level, because he was always active listening, repeating whatever Mikey would say.

Michael would say, "What's that Mikey? You want some dessert?"

And I'd say, "Sure Mikey, here're some cookies," and I'd put a half dozen cookies on a plate in the middle of the table. Michael would always nibble absently on a couple of the cookies while we talked, and then he would caution Mikey: "That's enough, Mikey. Remember, you're only allowed two cookies."

Except for the imaginary Mikey, Michael seemed to be getting better. He was starting conversations, talking about the news.

Then one Friday, almost two years after the accident, Michael started talking about women. Woman actually. Sharon, the waitress at the diner at the Navy Yard.

After pizza, we left Mikey to watch TV, and Michael and I went out on the balcony. He told me that he was going to ask Sharon out. I agreed to babysit Mikey.

But Michael struck out. He had asked her, "What time do you get off work?"

She'd said, "Seven," but Michael hadn't known what to say after that.

Michael needed help. "You nincompoop. Her answer meant she wanted a date. If she hadn't wanted a date, she'd have said "pretty late" or "my boyfriend's picking me up at seven."

So we planned it out.

The next time, Michael invited her to go to a movie with him after work. That was a "no," but she'd counter-offered for him to meet her for the early Mass that Sunday. Michael had said, "I'm not really a church kind of guy."

That was a complete nitwit thing for a guy to say if he's serious about a girl. Fortunately, Sharon hadn't been put off and she'd said, "I'll be there, regardless, and I'll keep a place for you." That was a good sign. Very good.

Now I'm not into dating any more, but I was getting a kick out of planning with Michael.

I helped Michael plot out the next step. He would go to the church. Not early. That way, she'd get there first and would worry if he was coming, and then she'd be relieved when he showed up. After church, he'd take her out to breakfast at Maggio's, and we put together a long list of things to talk about and questions to ask her. There was one possible problem. "Are you going to talk about the accident?"

"No, no, and if it comes up, I'll just say I don't want to talk about it."

"No," I said. "You want to act like you know each other really well. You should tell her, but if you can't, tell her there was a terrible accident, that you're still working out some of the issues, and you'll talk with her about it another time. The sooner you can talk to her about it, the better."

Early Sunday morning, Michael dropped Mikey off. We'd agreed that I would be the regular babysitter and that I would feed him healthy foods, watch only kids TV, and bedtime was seven. Michael also brought over books I could read to Mikey.

Sunday night around 6, there was a knock on my door. It was Michael and he barged right in.

"Hey, Mikey," he said, and then, "Sorry I'm late, Harry, but the date went real well."

"It was no trouble at all." I tried not to smile.

Then Michael started talking, talking so fast, it was hard to understand.

Just as the Mass had started, he'd been able to slide in right next to Sharon. She'd only looked at him once, but she'd stayed close, and moved her arm so that it pressed against his elbow. She hadn't moved away for the whole service. Michael had suggested Maggio's, like we'd planned, but she'd countered, "Let's get some bread and cheese, fruit, and Cokes from Crusoe's, and have a picnic in Prospect Park."

Michael had pretended he liked the idea and the date had gone fabulously well. "Harry," he said, eyes sparkling, "we spent the whole afternoon talking. She grabbed both my hands and looked right into my eyes. Like this." He grabbed my hands, looked right at me. "She called my name. I've never felt like this. Not even before, back when—"

"That's great," I interrupted, sparing him the pain of mentioning his dead wife.

So we got into a regular schedule. Michael, Mikey, and I still had our Friday night pizza. All day Sundays and then Wednesday night Mass was for Michael and Sharon with me babysitting Mikey. They were going slow and that was good.

Michael said he felt closer sitting next to Sharon in church than he ever had making out with any of those girls in the backseat of his Chevy back in Detroit.

There was no question about where it would go. Not for Michael, and it sounded like Sharon was just as serious. There was one major problem looming in the near future. Sharon didn't know that Michael had this delusion about Mikey.

"One problem," Michael told me one Friday night. "One little problem. Sharon wants to meet my friends and family. Now you're fine, I want her to meet you. But Mikey ..." Michael paused and looked down. "I just feel in my gut that there might be a problem. And I'm scared to death of losing Sharon."

I waited 'til he continued.

"Yeah, I know Mikey could be a problem. After the accident, things were awfully dark for a while until they told me that Mikey was going to be OK."

"You need Mikey. You think Sharon might not understand."

"Yeah. I know there's a problem about Mikey, but I can't even think about it. Eventually, we'll be able to talk it out. I'll be able to straighten everything out in my head."

This was progress. Michael was aware of the problem, sort of, and he was moving in the right direction.

"But Harry," he continued, "Sharon wants to meet Mikey now. How long can I put it off?"

"You can't put it off, Michael, or she'll think you're ashamed of her or you're hiding something."

"Yeah." He thought a while. "How about I bring her to see you first, then I'll go out on the balcony, and you tell her about Mikey. Then she and I can deal with it slow. Over a couple of months, maybe. She'll do that for me, Harry. We love each other. I love her so much ..." He looked down and took a long breath.

"OK," I said. It sounded like a good idea. "How about you bring her over for pizza on Friday?"

"No. What would I do with Mikey? We'll do it Thursday morning. I'll take a sick day, drop Mikey off at daycare, pick up Sharon, and bring her over here. We'll have plenty of time. Her work doesn't start 'til eleven."

Wednesday night, Michael called me. It was all set and it looked like things were starting to work out. It was about time. Sharon had been good for him and I figured Michael was on the road toward sanity.

Thursday morning I set everything up for entertaining. Hot water on the stove, Lipton's and Nescafe, regular and decaf on the counter. Saltines and cheddar on a plate. Door to the balcony open. At 8:45, there was a knock on the door. "Hey Harry, it's Michael. And Sharon."

I pulled open the door and there was Michael gesturing off to the side as he said, "Sharon, this is Harry, Harry this is ..."

I looked at the emptiness at Michael's side and couldn't stop my mouth from gaping as I stared at Michael's face, then back to the emptiness, then his face, back and forth, back and forth.

Michael looked over to his side where Sharon should have been and startled like he was seeing something for the first time or, in this case, *not* seeing something. He swept his arm where Sharon should have been. He looked behind him, then turned back, his eyes open wide. His mouth hung open. Our eyes met and his face contorted with a churning mixture of anger, fear, and despair.

Michael howled like he had at the funeral parlor three years before. He tried to shove past me and I grabbed his arm instinctively. He looked at the balcony and then back at me still howling.

Michael had lost everything. Twice. I'd been mentoring him so much that I kind of felt like it had happened to me. I stumbled against the doorjamb while Michael pulled away. He staggered out the door to the balcony and lifted a leg over.

Michael stopped howling five seconds later when he hit the ground. It struck me then: I had lost my best friend. I bent over and I started howling. I was still howling when the cops came.

Times were tough for the next couple of years.

It took some work, but things got better.

Mikey's done pretty well. He's in college now. Psych major at NYU, just across the Brooklyn Bridge in Manhattan, so he commutes. He takes the bus, not the train. My life would be pretty bleak without him.

Harry Demarest

the slow tango of flame and ember

by Kaz Sussman

Hail squalls feed the raku of black
ice crazing its way up the hill. The night
stirs a chaos of fallen leaves over the path

home. My hands have worked
both cedar and sunlight, building
this space that holds true at the axe edge
of winter, where the woodstove
whispers all is well. In its belly, oak boughs
to the slow tango of flame and ember.

In the cleaving cold beyond the windows
an unmeasured world burrows
into its future, and a glory
of pale frost hints of its travels.

Invasion of the Oldies

by Joyce Tomlinson

Day 1

Dad's first night with us, here while his wife, Donna, has surgery. He's in our bed, and Gary and I are attempting sleep in the guest room on the lower floor. The house noises are different in this room than the sounds I'm used to upstairs. I fade in and out of sleep, unsettled by the rumbling of the furnace and the wind rattling the window. I mistake a voice in my dreams for my father's, and wake up with adrenaline surging through my body, thinking he's calling me. Later when he actually does call out, I run up the stairs and find him in the hall, bare from the waist down, with his pajama bottoms in his hands.

"I peed my pants," he says. He's distressed, doesn't know why he's in this strange place, or where to find a toilet. When I guide him back into the bedroom, I walk through a trail of urine on the carpet where Dad has dribbled as he tried to find someone to help him. I fish through his suitcase for dry boxer shorts and fresh pajamas, trying to keep my eyes averted so I won't stare at his stick thin legs and bare bottom. I pull his walker close and we head across the slate floor of the master bath, which suddenly seems ridiculously large. I'm scared he won't make it to the toilet without collapsing.

Finally he is settled on the toilet, and I turn away to give him the illusion of privacy. Gary has joined me in the bathroom and waits with me for Dad to be finished. When we hear the metal walker begin to roll on the slate floor, we turn around. There is my father on his knees, his upper body draped across the walker and his head down, moving toward the bathroom door.

Gary and I each take an arm and try to lift him to his feet, but he fights us. He's groaning now, plodding slowly across the stone floor on his knees. He's saying he needs to go to the hospital, but when I ask him why, what's wrong, he is beyond hearing me. Finally he reaches the bed, still on his knees, and lays his head down on the mattress, his eyes closed. "You better call the doctor," he says. Somehow Gary is able to get him to his feet, and the two of us maneuver his legs up onto the bed. By now I am done in, and my father is in agony. I look at my husband and say, "We can't do this."

Day 2

The next morning, Dad has forgotten the night trauma. Gary goes out first thing to buy a bedside commode so there will be no more breakdowns in the wee hours caused by the distance to the toilet. I leave Dad in the care of the woman I hired as an aide and go to my home office to work. Gary drives off to his job an hour away. I've called to tell Pete, the owner of Senior Helpers, that we need someone on the night shift, and he promises help for tonight. The house is quiet, and I settle in to work. Finally, I'll be able to get some writing done.

A few hours later, I'm deep in thought when the day-shift nurse knocks on my office door. My father has slid out of bed and she can't get him up. When I reach him, Dad is lying on the floor with his knees drawn up to his chest. He's still wearing his pajamas and his eyes are closed. He's chilled; I pull the blankets off the bed and cover him up. He moans softly while the nurse and I discuss our options. We decide not to move him, in case he's broken a bone. Everything is okay, I tell him, I'm going to get some help. I dial 911 and within minutes my house is full of medics and firefighters and police officers.

I follow the ambulance to the emergency room. Gary meets me there. In the waiting room, I begin to shake. Not even 48 hours since taking responsibility for my dad, and he's fallen. What if he'd hit his head on the bedside table, what if he's broken a hip? I'm sobbing, but I know he'll be upset if he sees me cry, so I force myself to get control of my emotions. Someone comes to take us to his room in the ER, and by the time I reach his bedside, I'm able to smile.

After the exam, and the tests, and the okay from the ER doc that the fall hasn't done any damage to my fragile father, an orderly pushes him to the door in a wheelchair. Dad's dressed in slacks and a button-down shirt, in good spirits now, revived by all the solicitous attention and warm blankets. We stop at a restaurant for lunch on the way home, and Dad comments on the lovely view, the nice time he's had today.

Day 5

We've established the routine of dinner at 6:00 and a movie at 7:00. Dad is partial to Fred Astaire, so we've seen a string of old musicals with inane storylines and elaborate dance numbers. Dad sits next to me on the sofa, tapping his foot. Sometimes we sing along when he remembers the words.

In one film called *The Pleasure of His Company*, Debbie Reynolds plays Astaire's daughter, Jessica. Astaire's character, Pogo, is divorced from Jessica's mother, and he's been away traveling to exotic places for most of his daughter's life. In some scenes the similarities to my experience with my own father are mirrored so closely, I have to leave the room and shake off the sting. In one scene, Pogo tells Jessica, "I didn't give you much thought over the years," and I can't help saying aloud, "What a jerk."

Dad doesn't seem to register the comment.

I remember the one time Dad took me to see a movie when I was eight-years-old. The film, called *The Wreck of the Mary Deare*, centered on a ship found drifting at sea without a crew—an odd movie to take a little girl to see, dark and somewhat frightening. And yet I cherish that time, sitting next to my dad in the theatre as the lights dimmed, a giddy sensation in my belly as the opening credits began. The two of us watching the story play out together.

Now I turn to my Dad sitting next to me on the sofa, mesmerized by Pogo/Astaire even though he can't track the story. I reach over and take his hand in mine. "Do you remember going to see *The Wreck of the Mary Deare* with me when I was a kid?" I ask him. Immediately his expression changes. "No, no, I don't think so," he says. He pulls his hand away, his eyes cloud over, and I kick myself for asking. Every time his recall fails, it's another defeat for him, and an irrational disappointment for me.

Day 6

Several times a day I remind my father where he is. "I'm your daughter, Joyce," I say. "We're at my house." This morning while he was still in bed he asked, "What is this place?" and once again I started to say, "I'm Joyce, this is my bedroom." But before I could finish, he stopped me.

"This isn't a bedroom, this is a *palace*," he said, and all at once I saw my house, my life, through his eyes. He's always lived so frugally and now he sleeps in my imported, hand carved bed with the gas fireplace switched on and an adjoining marble bathroom so big he can't push a walker across without having an accident. What must he think of my choices, I wonder. What do *I* think of them?

He wants to go home. I tell him, "We're family and family sticks together," and wince at the irony of the words. But I look at him, so fragile, like he could break in two with the slightest bump. He needs me and this is the closet we've come in a long time to being a family sticking together.

Day 7

Donna's surgeon is in the doghouse. He saved her life, her cancer is completely eradicated, but he's committed the unforgivable crime of talking down to her.

Joyce Tomlinson

She repeats the phrase he used over and over with exaggerated sarcasm: "We've spent a *million* dollars trying to figure out that pain of yours." I know she's just had half a lung removed, but by the fifth or sixth repetition, I'm ready to give her wheelchair a forceful push down the nearest hill.

She's been released from the hospital and Gary and I drove in the city to pick her up while a nurse stayed with Dad. Once home, Donna parked her new walker next to Dad's two models: the convertible "transporter" he can sit on like a wheelchair and the stripped down, lightweight one. We now have what looks like a walker showroom with several canes leaned up against an adjoining wall and a portable oxygen tank next to the sofa. With the plastic shower chair, the bedside commode, and the revolving nurses, our house feels more like a nursing home every day.

Day 8

Despite being short of breath, Donna has been shooting orders at the aides all morning.

"Get him up and walk him down the hallway, " she demands. "He needs exercise! Has anyone been keeping track of his BMs?" She woke up before me and took charge of Dad's breakfast. We've been feeding him oranges when evidently what he needs is bananas. He likes Raisin Bran, not the Shredded Wheat we've foisted on him all week. She's made a list of groceries we didn't know we needed and sent Gary off to the store. I'm hiding out up in my office, trying to figure out the best time to sneak downstairs for another cup of coffee.

At the end of the day, the night nurse gets my Dad into bed, and I go in to say goodnight and kiss his cheek, as I've done each night since he's been with us. I've enjoyed this reversal of our tucking-in ritual from my pre-divorce childhood when Dad came in for a few minutes before lights out to tell me a story and say goodnight. I'd thought these moments were gone forever, and I've found myself prolonging them, pulling up the covers, patting his hand.

Tonight as I approach his side of the bed, Donna steps directly between my father and me. I fall back, startled, but Donna is oblivious; she continues whatever mission she's on. I feel my face redden, I hurry out of the room and stand trembling in the hallway. Suddenly, I am ten years old and my father has moved onto his boat; I am thirteen and he's just remarried. I slink down the stairs to the guest room, hanging on tight to the handrail, swallowing hard to stop the tears.

Day 16

We have settled into a routine. At eight each morning, the night caregiver hands over the reigns of the household to the day helper. The one who is leaving fills out a log of bowel movements and medications amid long discussions about the consistency of my father's poop and the frequency of its expulsion. Donna is now administering three different laxatives on the advice of three different caregivers, none of whom have a medical degree and all with accents thick enough that we struggle to understand. The rotating workers range in age from nineteen to sixty and many of them are devoutly Christian. Even Pete from Senior Helpers told me he was praying for us; I'm not sure whether to resent the intrusion of religion into what should be a professional relationship or grateful for any help I can get.

My house is beginning to smell like a nursing home, a combination of vegetable soup, stale air, and the pee-soaked Depends someone left in the trash. Airing the house has to be done surreptitiously—a window opened here and there—otherwise, I'm scolded for trying to freeze the oldies, in spite of the blazing fire and cranked up thermostat. Gary and I peel off layers of clothing trying to cool off while Dad and Donna pile on blankets.

My father has fallen three more times since the emergency room visit. Each tumble he's taken has happened as he hoisted himself out of bed; his legs crumple underneath him and he lands with a thud on the bedroom carpet. Donna has taken to overseeing the aides as they lift Dad back up while I busy myself in another part of the house and try not to think about what's happening in my old bedroom.

Day 20

Pete has become so comfortable coming and going from my house that this morning he walked in without knocking. Every day, rotating caregivers traipse through our normally quiet home, rummage through our pantry and turn on ESPN to watch sports. Since Donna moved in, I leave the movies to the oldies after dinner and lie low in my office.

Last night, Gary stopped me in the hallway and whispered, "Meet me in the exercise room at nine o'clock." A few minutes before nine, I said goodnight to the oldies and their caregiver, all lined up on the sofa watching *Roman Holiday* with Audrey Hepburn and Gregory Peck. Dad barely looked up when I gave him a kiss on the cheek. Even though he can't follow the story, he sure thinks that Hepburn girl is a dish.

Joyce Tomlinson   51

"I'm going downstairs to read," I said to the room and dashed down the stairs, a bit like a delinquent teenager sneaking out of the house. Inside the exercise room, a bottle of wine and two glasses sat balanced on the bench press, a bag of Erin's popcorn on the floor between two folding chairs. Gary had queued up an episode of The Voice on the big screen and sat waiting for me with a conspiratorial smile on his face.

I sat down with my husband but shifted and squirmed. I could get away with slipping away to read—I *had* to read for school. But a guilty-pleasure TV show? I stuffed a handful of popcorn in my mouth and washed it down with wine. What if there was an emergency upstairs while we were down there in the basement getting buzzed? Dad could fall again or, God forbid, *die right there in the T.V. room.*

I paused the show to listen for movement upstairs. I could only hear muffled movie dialogue, nothing out of the ordinary. I took another sip of wine. The caregiver could handle anything that came up, right? Either he or Donna could be down here in seconds if they need us.

Just then we heard a knock. I jumped to my feet, and staggered slightly as I headed for the door. Jeez, I thought, pull yourself together. This is exactly why you shouldn't be down here drinking. Oh my god, if anything has happened ...

I flung open the door and there stood Donna with the remote control in her hand, unable to figure out how to rewind. While Gary explained the remote buttons to her for the third time that day, she peered past him into the exercise room, taking in the drained wine glasses, the almost empty bottle, the popcorn spilled on the floor between the folding chairs.

Surely I shouldn't be too ashamed to meet her eyes.

Day 36

Now that Donna has recuperated from her surgery, we're moving the oldies to a one-bedroom apartment at Aegis Assisted Living. I'm sitting with Dad while the manager walks Donna through the paperwork. Dad's legs look like twigs in sweat pants. The fringe of white hair around his baldhead is so long and haywire, he could be a mad scientist. His nails have gown out past his fingertips and he's got drips of lunch all down his front. I want to take him for a quick haircut, change his shirt. Fix him somehow. Make him back into the strong, alert man he was at forty, only sweet, like this older version. If he'd just snap out of his senility and become lucid again, even for a day.

Dad nods off repeatedly and, each time he comes to, he demands to go home. When I remind him that he and Donna are staying here, that his house has too many stairs for him to climb, he looks puzzled. He says he doesn't remember their place having any stairs at all. Now I wonder if he's picturing *my* house and *that's* where he wants to be.

Donna insists this move is temporary, just until Dad gets the strength back in his legs. I'm careful not to oversell; I accept her terms. She's signed the two of them up for 16 days of respite care. After that, I don't know where she thinks they're going.

Day 37

Our house is empty. No more patients, no caregivers. The medical equipment is gone, the canes and oxygen tanks have been cleared out, the bedside commode and shower chair are in storage. We're back to sleeping in our own bed, using our own shower. One minute I'm relishing the solitude, the next I miss the clank and scrape of Dad's walker across the hardwood floor.

Last night around nine o'clock, I got a call from the nurse on staff at Aegis. Seems earlier in the evening my father took off down the sidewalk trying to get home or wherever he thought home was. Two aides followed close behind him, he didn't get too far. All was well in the end. They just wanted to let me know.

I hung up and began to pace. What if he'd fallen on the sidewalk or gotten lost? Walking away might be a sign that his condition is deteriorating. I've heard dementia patients can get worse when they're relocated. At what point might Aegis decide he needs to move into Memory Care, the facility next door where they lock the doors and restrain the patients?

By the morning, I'd begun to see the inevitability of Dad's jailbreak. He'd probably already forgotten about the month he spent at my place. He might not remember the house he built with the thirty-two stairs, or even his sailboat, without being prompted. But he did know he wanted to leave that place. We should've known he'd try. He never was the kind of man to stick around once he got the itch to roam.

Bay Leaves

by Graham Murtaugh

She surprises with her trust:
opening her mouth
to the fist he holds out
full of bay leaves.

They take the dare
together: chewing a heady mouthful
plucked from an ordinary tree.
What remedy, what memory?

The spice startles. Takes them
to a small kitchen in Lisbon.
A widow with eleven children
sips pale tea.

A simple table and chair.
White walls. An arched window
and afternoon shadow. A weary smile plays.
The scent is stronger, somehow.

In the yard, their hands drop.
She goes to boil water. He stands
in the warm sun, in the shade
of Oregon myrtle trying to recall

the Portuguese for great thankfulness
but knowing only the words for fruit
and simple colors—blue and green—
for stars and salt.

InterMedium

by Richard Beckham II

Midmorning, on a Tuesday, Edward Baxter leisurely strolled down to the posh part of his neighborhood known as the Village. His plan was to sit in a small café and quietly eat and drink among his newlywed and nearly dead neighbors.

He passed women out walking dogs, who passed other women out walking themselves. They all seemed to know each other. One woman in a blue jumpsuit passed Ed and said, "Hi." He froze, not sure of what to do.

When he walked past the drugstore, he watched oversized cars with disabled parking placards and "baby on board" signs try to navigate the cramped parking lot, nearly bumping into each other in the process. White-haired, cane-limping men and women slowly stepped out of those shiny machines alongside women in yoga pants who sprung out of their luxury vehicles. As Ed watched this typical scene in the drugstore parking lot he told himself that he should stop by there on his way back home to get some snacks.

But before he crossed the next crosswalk, he saw a penguin-footed woman wobble across the street, waving at another woman about her age. This other woman carried a cloth bag spilling over with fruits and vegetables. The penguin woman stopped in the middle of the crosswalk as a giant moving truck grinded to a halt right beside her. She and her friend met in the middle of the street without noticing the truck and then headed towards the drugstore together.

Ed went inside a café that smelled of espresso, chocolate, and baked bread. A little bell jingled above the door as he entered. At a table by the window were six senior citizens, only one of which was a man. The women talked and the man chimed in when he felt it necessary.

"I remember," one of the women said. "Ira had a limousine. It was one of those big long limousines with all the seats in it and the champagne. I couldn't believe that she got one of those with all the seats. I mean it was nice, but my stars, there was only four of us. I mean ..."

Ed walked up to the counter and looked at the menu scrawled in colored chalk on the blackboard.

"Ira's just showing off," the man said, flapping his newspaper. "You know how she is."

The women nodded and looked over at Ed.

A man that reminded Ed of a Norse god strode out of the kitchen. He told Ed that somebody would help him in a second. A second later an androgynous person with cropped red Kool-Aid hair came out and asked what he'd like.

"Wait a minute," the person said. "Are you Ed Baxter?"

"Yeah." He smiled and could feel the women behind him staring. They whispered not very quietly.

"I didn't know you lived so close," Kool-Aid said.

"Yep. Pretty close."

"What's that thing that you invented called again?"

Ed told her it was called InterMedium then he ordered a foamy coffee and an egg and spinach sandwich. He sat by the door and watched the pale Viking shoot steam into his coffee.

One of the women at the other table smiled and waved to him. She got up to go over to his table. The man stood to make room. Chairs squealed against the floor. The old woman came over, smiled politely, then said, "Remember me?" She had a toad in her throat.

The other women leaned in towards each other and whispered. The man pretended to read his newspaper.

"We talked at the grocery store a couple weeks ago. Then at the gas station before that, I think." She smiled and pointed at herself. "Beth."

Ed said, "That's right, Beth."

Kool-Aid set a plate down on Ed's table as Beth began to take a seat across from him. "Mind if I sit down?" she said after she was already sitting.

Ed told himself that he could still leave his house and feel free whenever he wanted.

"Did you give any more thought to meeting my granddaughter? She's very pretty, you know. And very smart. Like you. She majored in biochemistry and graduated with honors. Smart as a whip, I tell you."

"No, I didn't know she graduated with honors. Good for her." The Norseman set down Ed's coffee in front of Beth.

"I made one of those afterlife profiles on that InterMedium program of yours, since I last saw you," Beth said. "There were so many questions to set it up though and so many videos that I had to make. But I guess it's worth it to be able to talk to people after I'm gone. Like my granddaughter. She helped me, Amy, that's her name. Smart as a whip, I tell you. I think the two of you would make a cute couple. I know you probably hear that a lot, but I really mean it. I have an eye for those things." She glanced over at the women gossiping by the window. "I can spot couples that have a chance of making it." She leaned in. "Her last boyfriend," she shook her head, "not a chance. That was probably her only boyfriend. In college, if I can remember."

The little bell jingled and a young woman jammed a stroller through the door. Kool-Aid gave the woman a big smile and a loud greeting.

"Do you have a pen?" Beth said.

"A pen? No, no, I don't have a pen. I have my phone."

"Okay then. Here, let me give you her number. You're too handsome and successful not to have a girlfriend, Edward. Really. Amy's very down to Earth. I think you two would get along. And I'm not just saying that." She gave Ed her granddaughter's number. "Give her a call. Or send her a text, like you kids do. It would be good for the both of you. Well, toodle-oo." Beth got up and went back over to her friends. She gave Ed a little wave of her hand. He thought she was sweet.

After Ed finished his coffee and ate his sandwich, he left and headed for the drugstore. As he crossed the street, he heard two women talking loudly.

"It's important, Joan. You've got to keep moleskin in the house. For blisters. I mean you never know when they'll show up or who needs them."

"I know," Joan said. They nearly walked on Ed's heels as they went across the parking lot without looking for roving vehicles. "I'm pretty sure I have some in the cupboard, as a matter of fact," she went on. "Or maybe it's in the closet by the bathroom. I try to keep it in the house. I really do try."

A man in sweatpants with wild greasy hair entered the drugstore before Ed. Ed watched him fill a tote basket with stacks and stacks of beans, chilies, and soups. After Ed picked out some sunflower seeds and tortilla chips, he headed for the long line at the check-stand. When it was Ed's turn, a woman appeared out of nowhere with a toilet brush and stepped in front of him. She started chit-chatting with the cashier about somebody in the hospital. The cashier waved Ed up to the counter and the woman with the toilet brush slinked away and went to the back of the line.

On his way home, Ed watched a spotless viridian Jaguar carefully parallel park in a spot that could easily fit an RV and decided to get a hold of Amy. The excursion on that Tuesday midmorning got him to realize that he needed a change from the type of people he interacted with regularly.

The mansion, or what Ed called his "Mans," had a subterranean floor with a theater room and two dozen leather seats equipped with their own cooler and seat warmer. Each of the Mans' three floors had balconies, which overlooked the bay of the city. A universal sound system set up in every room created the ambiance of a luxury hotel. The master bedroom had a shower large enough for a basketball team. On the roof, a small garden with herbs and flowers sat off to the side of a shuffleboard court and fire pit. Air Force grade glass tables and chairs made up the lawn furniture. The same glass was used for the walls, floor, and ceiling of his home office; though on the outside, the glass was completely reflective, even at night.

Ed unlocked the front gate and door of the Mans with a fingerprint scanner. He sat in a living room chair that could easily fit a male buffalo. That was where he sent a text to Amy. This led to a series of texts and became the means that they got to know one another over the next few days.

They agreed to meet up for a drink at a restaurant downtown. The restaurant had very high ceilings with a winding tower of wine bottles at its vortex. The bar was close to the ceiling, in the back, up a long straight flight of stairs.

Ed made sure to arrive first so that they would have a table with a view of the people dining below in dresses and sport coats. Another patron recognized him and told him that InterMedium was a big sham, like all the other psychics that made money off the misfortunes of others. But there was perfume in the air that mixed with the occasional steamy broth of clams. Every three feet or so were small tea light candles in frosted globes to offset the darkly painted walls and floors. Ed was watching the dancing candlelight on his table when Amy arrived.

She was petite. Her hair was dark and her skin youthful. She didn't look anything like Ed imagined. Her eyes were quick and her reactions were graceful. They shook hands then sat in high heavy chairs. They ordered wine and fried calamari and began their conversation with quips about their appearances.

"This is the first time I've worn this jacket," Ed said. "I don't really dress up that much."

"I kind of figured from the pictures I've seen of you on TV. I'm sorry. I didn't mean to bring that up. I didn't want to make things awkward."

"No don't worry about. I'm sure that most people know who I am and what I look like. It's fine. But I'm just a normal guy."

"I'm sure you are. I'm not the kind of person who gets star-struck, you know. I ran into Robert Cicero once. I mean I *literally* ran into him." She laughed a little. Ed liked the sound of her laugh and how her cheeks punctuated her eyes in the frosted candlelight. "I was coming out of the bookstore on campus and I bumped into him. I got all flustered. I don't know what I said. But he was nice and kept walking. I think he was doing a book signing or something. For a memoir, maybe, since he's an actor and all. He was probably just going home after that. I think he lives here in the city, doesn't he? Do you know him?"

"No, I never met him," Ed said. Then the calamari arrived and they talked about where they grew up and how they were both teased in school.

"You didn't even make the football team?" she said. "I thought they let anybody on the football team. At least that's what they did at my school."

"I mean I never played. I would suit up for games and stuff and get all warmed up, but they'd never let me do even one play. Even when we were winning 85-7."

They ate warm bread along with the calamari and drank glass after glass of Napa Valley wine.

"So," she said. "I have to ask. How did you come up with the idea of a website that you could talk to dead people with?"

"Okay. I don't really tell anybody this, but—" Ed swirled his wine "—I was watching a movie with my grandpa when I was about ten years old. It was some older movie and they were using those landline phones and a bunch of other old stuff, so I asked him questions about all of it." He took a sip. "He answered me for a while, but then he stopped. It turned out that he passed away when we were watching the movie together. While I was talking to him."

"Oh my God. That's terrible."

They both held the stems of their wine glasses, the reflection of the candlelight made the wine look black.

"So, yeah, that's how I got the idea. Then I started working on the program when I was twenty in college, then it went live and the rest is history."

"Like," she said. "Wait, like that law they named after you. Didn't they name a law after you?"

"Edward's Law, yeah. They were going to call it Baxter's Law but I guess they already had a law with that name."

"What's that about again? Like how if somebody wrote a will then that will would nullify anything that the afterlife profile says about inheritance?"

Ed nodded and thought about his own afterlife profile on InterMedium. The night went on and their laughter loosened. Whenever Amy asked questions about what it was like to be famous, Ed reminded himself of what Beth had said about her. And the more he reminded himself of this, the more beautiful Amy became.

That first date turned into other dates, which turned into watching movies together. First at her condo and then eventually at the Mans. Ed tried out the term to Amy while he showed her around. She thought it was funny and cute, like all his witticisms. After Amy had stayed the night a few times at the Mans, Ed began to become aware that it was harder for him to imply that she should leave when he wanted her to.

"Well, I should probably do some work in the snow globe," he said while they reclined on his ten-person couch and watched the world news.

"Snow globe?" She laughed a little. "It's alright. I don't have to do any work until later." So she stayed on the couch and watched his satellite TV. Ed paused a couple seconds before he got up and went to his office to work. His employees saw him only over the computer. Some even joked that maybe his afterlife profile ran the company.

Months later, on a Saturday, Ed and Amy were out eating salmon scrabbles for breakfast when she got a call from her mom. Beth had been hit by a train. They said that she most likely stopped on the tracks to make sure that there was no train coming. Amy broke down over her scramble and blew her nose into a napkin. Ed tried to console her, but couldn't do so in the restaurant, so he asked the waitress to box up their food.

Ed went to the funeral with Amy and bought a dozen white roses for the occasion. At the wake, people asked him if he was Ed Baxter and he only nodded in reply. About two weeks later, Amy asked Ed a question as she cooked breakfast topless in the en suite kitchen of the master bedroom.

"What do you think about me moving in here with you?" she said.

"Oh yeah?" His face became hot.

"Yeah. I think it'd be good. Plus it's time we move forward. Don't you think? We've been together for almost a year and things are going pretty good."

"It would be something," he said. "But what about the job offer you just got? Wasn't there a chance of you relocating?"

"Oh, I decided against that."

"But doesn't your job not like that you're looking around?"

"Yeah," she said, flipping over the eggs.

"What, they don't care?"

"They let me go. That was, umm, about five days ago. Last week, maybe."

Ed watched her finish cooking but didn't say anything.

Amy sold her condo the next month and moved into the Mans. Ed thought of Beth and believed that, deep down, Amy had a good heart. He had seen proof in more ways than one: in how she donated money to the victims of tragedies they saw on TV and how she gave leftovers to the homeless when they ate downtown.

Ed enjoyed having somebody to keep him company, especially somebody who laughed at his corny jokes. He began to enjoy spending time with her so much that he started not to update his afterlife profile as often. When he first noticed this, he thought of his future children. So one of his last updates around this time went:

Okay immortal twin. I've now realized that love is the most important thing. And that it's important to trust people and open your heart to them. It's a good thing, trust me. It really is. Like if you find somebody that makes you happy and they're genuine, then you have to go for it. And don't look back. That's why I've decided to ask Amy if she'll marry me. I want to share everything with her. It'd make me happy because it'd make her happy. Then happiness grows from happiness to make even more happiness and that's what I think it's all about.

Ed Baxter asked his CFO to go to a jewelry store for him to get the ring. The CFO took pictures of rings in the store with his phone and sent them to Ed while he was in his snow globe. They unanimously decided on a three-carat diamond solitaire. In order to get the ring size Ed hired a jeweler to come by the Mans while Amy was out shopping.

For the proposal, Ed's plan was to take Amy to a cliff that overlooked the wide gorgeous bay of the city and to have a string quartet hide behind some trees and play "Canon in D" by Pachelbel.

"So it's all set?" Ed said to one of his assistants via videophone in his glass office.

"Yep, they'll be there at noon. Hiding and waiting for your signal."

"And they'll be dressed formally?"

"Yeah, they'll be dressed formally. They probably won't like to wait too long because it's supposed to be a scorcher. But they'll be there."

"Good," Ed said proudly, "because it's all got to go as planned. It's very important that it all goes to plan."

Ed stood with a smile and left his office to gaze upon his bride-to-be with a new pair of eyes. He thought that she was in the living room on the second floor because the TV was on, but she wasn't there. Something in his heart told him not to use the intercom to find her. So instead he went from room to room, holding onto the smile that had formed in the glass office.

Amy was in the library, which contained books neither she nor Ed had read

Richard Beckham II

nor heard of. She was on her laptop at a mahogany desk, in a chair upholstered with green leather. Ed approached her quietly from the threshold and noticed that she was on InterMedium. He recognized Beth's voice on the laptop and saw Beth's face on the screen. His first instinct was to walk softly and tuck away his smile.

"He's a good one now," Beth's afterlife profile said. "I hope you didn't let him get away and that you followed my plan and trusted me as my dying wish. I know what's best for you, you know."

"No, grandma, everything's fine. I moved in with him. Things are good."

"Did you give to the needy when he was around like I told you to do? Did it work?"

"Yep, like a charm. I just wanted to say thank you for all the advice and that I miss you. I even think he's planning on—" Her head spun around.

Ed, on the verge of tears, put his hands out to reach for something to brace himself with.

"Ed! I'm sorry. I'm sorry. You weren't supposed to find out this way." She went over to him but he pushed her away and left the room.

Amy slept in a bedroom without its own kitchen that night. While she was there, Ed sent her a text:

"You have to move out tomorrow. I've notified a moving company. You should probably tell your mom."

Amy broke into tears and thought of her grandmother. She moved out the next day and did not see Ed because he locked himself in the snow globe. For hours, he sat in his plush desk chair, looking at the solitaire ring and his view of the city until the sun set.

The string quartet had to be paid but they did not have to hide on top of the cliff in the heat. A few days after Amy moved out, Ed decided to go up to the cliff with the amazing view of the bay where he was to propose to Amy. He took the ring with him.

At about noon, he slowly walked through the park and looked at the green leaves of the trees and the couples with arms around each other's waists. The birds chirped and the flowers enticed dozens of bees. But Ed wore sunglasses and a baseball cap to hide his eyes. A few people stood by the wooden fence on the cliff's ledge when he got there. He twirled the ring in his pocket and waited patiently for them to leave.

While he waited, he surveyed the bay and how it glistened in the sun. The few people that were also admiring the view picked up on Ed's wish to be alone and they walked off. Ed leaned against the fence and sighed deeply, taking the ring from his pocket. He looked at it one last time and glanced down the steep cliff below.

As he started to hurl the ring over the cliff, he noticed somebody right behind him. He was caught off guard and dropped the ring. His ankle twisted under the fence and he lost his balance. He jumped backwards, startled by who he saw.

"Ed!" Amy shouted as she watched him tumble over the fence. People ran over to help but it was too late. Amy picked up the ring.

Edward Baxter's family flew in from Key Largo for the funeral. In his ambition to create InterMedium he did not make a Last Will and Testament, so his parents inherited the estate. Shortly after the funeral, they activated Ed's afterlife profile. His immortal twin told them about his love for Amy and how he wanted her to have everything that was his. They felt moved by his uncharacteristic turn of affection and so they gave Amy the Mans and a quarter of his wealth.

In those early months, Amy became the target of paparazzi, but the obsession quickly dissolved. She wore the three-carat solitaire ring every day and although she never married she adopted and raised seven children in the Mans. Before bed, on most nights, she went into the glass office to keep Ed's immortal twin up-to-date on the children and to talk to him about their future and their past together. Sometimes the children asked him about old movies they saw.

Untitled 1967

Mark Rothko
Portland Art Museum, 2013

by Elizabeth McLagan

Whether one calls to the first washes of paint
as orange or salmon, whether the ragged

cloud and uneven square is a soiled brown
or black fading black, this is the year

the chapel murals are packed away, the year
he takes the family west by train and along

the way points out to his daughter the desert
colors he loves, and here, again, in April,

sun oils the wet leaves and puddles, so
the painting's splash could be mud, maybe

the drips and patches skin blotched in cold,
as when one ventures without a coat or umbrella

in light's first glint of heat and is caught
in shadow or downpour, and here, and here

the morning's coffee and quince, the blossoms
nearly celestial, nearly twin to the plums

of the chapel, which is how the day is opening,
a gold onrushing spooled in a thread of train

speed, a labyrinth of pain and unknowing,
brown wheels, orange smoke, burn and a blessing.

Clinton Kelly, Cascadian Man

by Graham Murtaugh

Clinton Kelly Comes West

Clinton Kelly made much of our fair city. A scion, a bright star hung in the East. It's said he smelled of rosewater and leather, that he had not an unctuous bone in his body. He came from Clifty Creek, Pulaski County, Kentucky. He married thrice, sired fifteen children and named his sons to last: Archon, Calmet, Richmond, Penumbra. Let's do the same! *Well hello there, Shadow-Son.* Dear, stand in the October light with your shirt up: that dark-bellied ball is he, hiding in plain sight, destined for greatness.

Clinton Kelly in the Oregon Country

Slavery and hard-pan and broken Mother Church drove him West. His love of men was a goad, a glory-serpent snapping at his heels. Dust and privation filled his lungs, the bread of hunger filled his pocket. Fat and happy we wander the empty grounds of his fallen settler's home. Stone walls worn like old teeth. The same spirit breathes in us, small foot of life lashing out against your abdomen. After spring rains his grave blooms with flowers, a thousand yellow beacons at the center.

Clinton Kelly Goes Down to the Crossroads

Clinton Kelly and his rheumatism, his leathered preacher's hands, the brisk cut-cane walking into a prairie wind. His tee-totaling abolitionism cost him three wives, all told. How many shovels he must have handled. I wonder once you've drifted off, cozy in the pit of my chest and right arm, if Clinton Kelly ever lingered at the crossroads. Ever lit a midnight lantern, licked his fingers in the dark. Salt on his tongue. Foolishly, I try to count the same stars he knelt under, my countenance pale by the rising moon.

Clinton Kelly on the Mount of Transfiguration

It was too late; he was dead by then. But Plympton, his oldest boy, named it after the illuminated hill in Old Palestine. Christ came there to be lifted up, and so Father Kelly. Buried at the crest. Now we linger there under shade trees, looking out on the transfigured city, where the poor and dying suffer and know him not. Autumn leaves fallin a flurry, orange and yellow, a curtain of light. At a picnic shelter, a *quinceañera* is underway. We pause a moment to admire the young woman, twirling circles in her shimmering gown. So impossibly happy. We walk on.

The Workout Artist

by Geronimo G. Tagatac

❝Is that guy still in your aerobics class?" Denise asked my wife, Anthea.

"Which guy?" Anthea replied.

"*Which guy!*" said Denise, mocking my wife's reply. "The one with the drop-dead beautiful body who always takes the left front spot in class. The one half the women wanted to hire as their personal trainer."

I looked over at Denise's husband, Frank, who looked back at me, rolled his eyes, and rested his big right hand on the gentle slope of his stomach. "I knew a guy like that once. He didn't have a pot to piss in."

"You know the one I'm talking about," said Denise, ignoring her husband.

"Cecilio. Yes, he still comes to class," said Anthea, leaning back into her chair and staring straight into Denise's brown eyes. The sound of my wife's voice was as cool as steel. I looked at Denise. She had heard it too.

Breaking eye contact with me, Denise turned to Frank. "It wouldn't do you any harm to work out," she said, putting her hand over his.

"Yeah, maybe I could hire '*The Bod*,' as my personal trainer," he replied, emphasizing "Bod" with a mocking falsetto.

That night, when Anthea was asleep, I rose and went down the hall, away from the sound of her breathing. I went through the kitchen, where the copper pots and pans hung from the rack above the large marble counter, through the dining room, and into the living room, where I crossed the islands that the Persian carpets made on the oak floor. I tried to remember the young woman my wife had been in the first fall days I had known her. I tried to see her quick blue eyes and to hear her easy laughter. It was hard to erase the years of arguments between us, to sweep away the pile of harsh, cutting words over money, laundry, cereal brands, and vacation destinations.

I first saw her playing fiddle with the Bad Dog Jug Band, at a folk music club called the Off Stage Theater. I remembered the high, sweet sound of her voice and the soft sway of her body when they played *Long Train Gone*. I remembered the hot nights when our legs ate up miles of sidewalk, those times when we sent our voices and dreams flying toward each other in small restaurants and cheap cafés.

I walked over to the large west window. Miles away, the coastal range bulked

67

against the night. I had worked fourteen years for this view, these carpets, the thick lawns, and the teak patio furniture. I remembered how Anthea and I had laughed like two kids who'd broken into someone else's place on the day we moved in. We didn't even have enough furniture for most of the rooms. Now we owned two cars that were less than eighteen-months old and I was tied to a mortgage that would be with me until I was in my sixties. And what had it come to? I asked myself. My wife had the hots for a young guy with a nice body, a girl's name, and the future of a pair of sweat socks. The air around me tasted bitter.

In that moment I regretted love. I saw it for the seductive prison that it was. Why hadn't I said goodbye to Anthea on the day we graduated from college and gone off hitchhiking across Europe with my friend, Marty? I could have remembered her forever as she was. Below me on the dark carpet of lawn, the ghost of who I might have been stood. He was slim and strong, in jeans and a T-shirt, a backpack resting easily on his shoulders and hips. He looked up at me and smiled.

I reached over with my left hand and grasped my right bicep. Its hardness had disappeared years ago. I strained every time I had to take the garbage down the driveway to the edge of the street and I always returned out of breath from the short climb back up to the house. I glanced down at the curve of my stomach. At forty, I was on the fast track to middle age. And now, I was about to cross into cuckoldom. What a sorry, stupid joke it had all turned out to be.

Out of a deep, cold part of my mind an idea surfaced that made me laugh softly to myself.

"I hear you have a personal trainer called Cecilio," I said to the heavyset young woman who sat behind the counter at the Y. She closed her battered copy of *The Portable Kafka*, leaving her index finger in the page she'd been reading and said, "Yeah, he's good if you can get him."

"Is he available?"

"I don't know," she said, sliding a small notepad toward me. "Leave your name and phone number and I'll give it to him."

I wrote down my office number. "Do you have his number?"

She smiled at me as though I'd said something funny.

The voice over the phone was soft and pitched higher than I thought Cecilio's voice would be. "I train people to do a modified bodybuilder's workout. It's three times a week for the first month. You'll need an hour-and-a-half for each session," he said. "After the first month we'll go to five days a week."

The bastard's trying to scare me off, I thought. "Mornings or evenings?"

"Your choice. It's your dime."

"Six," I said. "How much do you charge?"

"A hundred a month for the first month. A hundred and fifty when we go to the full routine."

"When do we start?"

"Tomorrow morning."

"Morning?" I asked.

"You said six."

"I meant *after work*."

I heard him laugh. "Okay, see you in the weight room. Wear something that you can move in. Shorts, sweats, workout shoes."

Part of me was frightened of who I'd see in Cecilio. Maybe he was what every man feared in a rival, especially one whose childless marriage had gone politely silent for the last three years. Had Anthea first been drawn to this man by his almost whispery voice? Maybe it was simply the way he looked at her. Or perhaps it was a sudden lust at the first sight of his body, the same bawdiness I'd heard in Denise's voice when she talked about him. Once upon a time, I'd heard it in Anthea's voice as we lay together. I wondered if Cecilio was taller than me.

I'd never been in a real weight room. My high school gym had a bench press station and a few dumbbells. The weight plates had been the cheap plastic covered ones and the bars of black-painted pipe. That was a day-care center compared to this place. There were long racks of black iron dumbbells that went up, in five-pound increments, to one-hundred-and-ninety pounds. Standing in front of them, I couldn't imagine how anyone could pull them off their racks let alone use them. The bars for the bench presses were chromed steel at their ends. Where one's hands went, they were scored. They must have weighed twenty pounds all by themselves. The room had three bench press stations. I counted the plates at one of them and did the math in my head: more than eight hundred pounds. The cable machines with their tall, silver-painted weight stacks stood silently. All the way around the room were eight-foot mirrors and the floor was covered in black rubber matting. It was an unforgiving place.

I looked at myself in one of the mirrors. The bulk of the sweatshirt and the sweatpants exaggerated the shape of my body. For a moment, I thought that I was looking at a stuffed toy caricature of myself.

Geronimo G. Tagatac 69

"You Victor?"

I put my hands on my hips and stood still, forcing him to come to me. The man who came across the black floor was not tall. He was a few inches shorter than me. I could feel the thick calluses on his fingers and palm when I shook his hand.

"Cecilio Santos," he said.

"Victor," I replied.

He wore a full set of black sweats that were softer and more worn than mine. They looked freshly laundered. Their soft bulk could not disguise the depth of his chest and the width of his shoulders. When he brought his arm up to shake my hand, I saw motion beneath the front of his sweatshirt, the lower part of which hung loose. He must have had a twenty-eight-inch waist. I looked into his eyes again. Beneath the calm appraisal, I saw a sad toughness that I'd seen in people who have suffered the loss of a child or the betrayal of a lover. Whatever it was had stamped itself on Cecilio's face and left its mark around his eyes and the line of his mouth. He was at least as old as I was.

His high cheekbones could have been Asian or American Indian. His was not the deeply tanned face of someone who has spent his life outdoors. There was an ambiguity to his features, a mixing of shades generations old. I noticed unevenness in the left side of his head, a faint crease at his temple where the shadows seemed to gather to escape the neon light. His thick, black hair was parted on the left and cut nearly as short as mine. He looked at me with his unflinching brown eyes, sizing me up, estimating how long I would last. There was no hint of recognition in his eyes.

"Ever lifted before?" He asked.

"High school."

He nodded. "We'll work on form this week. No plates, just bars."

Resentment simmered in me. "Why can't I just start lifting?"

"I've got to teach you form."

"We're just pushing iron, not playing golf," I said.

Cecilio stared back at me, his face a quiet, dark pool. "Here," he said, "form is everything."

I wondered if the melodramatic son-of-a-bitch had used that line on my wife.

"Did you hurt yourself or something?" Anthea asked me over breakfast the next morning.

"I think I slept the wrong way. My back's a little stiff." I reached for the coffee pot, forcing myself not to wince at the pain that flared in the muscles of my right arm and shoulder. Mentally, I cursed Cecilio.

"You got back late yesterday," she said.

"Things have picked up at the office."

I searched her pale blue eyes for a hint of suspicion. Her eyes cut away from me as she poured milk into her cereal bowl.

"How about you? How're things at work?"

She picked up her spoon and held it suspended a few inches above the table-top. "The new boss is a pain. One of those anal types who thinks that if he can't see you, you're not working."

"Yeah," I said, trying to sound sympathetic.

"I try to make as many client calls as I can. Keeps me out of the office."

"Thank God for noon aerobics," I said.

"We'll start adding weights next week," Cecilio told me in the locker room on Friday. "Nothing big, just enough to work your muscles a little more."

"Do we go to five days?"

"Not for another four weeks."

"Here you go," I held a check out to him.

"You don't have to pay me till the end of the month."

"Take it. It'll be an incentive for me to come back on Monday."

Cecilio smiled and took the check without looking at it. "You still sore?"

"Not like I was on Tuesday." I felt a sudden satisfaction. I owned a part of him for a hundred measly dollars. I'll beat you both, I thought.

"Do you train many people?" I asked.

"Three besides you."

"Seems like a hard way to make a living," I replied, wondering if he was including my wife.

"It keeps me in protein powder," he said.

Anthea and I went to brunch at Don Juanito's with Frank and Denise the following Saturday. It was an upscale Mexican restaurant with a terra cotta tiled floor and a mesquite grill. The waiter had just taken our orders when Denise looked over at Anthea and said softly, "Hey."

On the far side of the restaurant, Cecilio, dressed in whites, had just emerged from the kitchen's door. He carried an empty bus tub in one hand. As soon as I saw his full-length white apron I knew that, in the restaurant hierarchy,

Cecilio was the lowest of the low: a dishwasher. He moved with the relaxed, almost slow-motion stride of a man who knows he has a long day of lifting and carrying ahead of him. His were not the movements of a desk worker for whom physical work is a break in the day's routine but those of a man whose body is a second voice.

Cecilio bent over to pick up an overflowing bus tray and when he straightened up, it might have been empty for all of the effort his face showed. I could see the veins rise into sharp relief against the skin of his forearms and his biceps bulged suddenly beneath the short sleeves of his white shirt. The muscles of his chest made the front of his shirt go taut. The gray plastic tub full of glasses, silverware, and plates must have weighed close to forty pounds.

I had a moment of panic. In my mind, I saw him cross the floor and hear his soft voice say, "Hey Victor. Gonna see you Monday?" His eyes would flash with realization and his face would freeze when he saw Anthea sitting next to me.

From across the dining room, his dark eyes swept over us but they registered nothing. There was no pause in his movement. Cecilio turned, strode across the room, and disappeared through the door to the kitchen.

I looked over at Anthea, whose face was as calm as the water in her green glass. I glanced at Denise. Her eyes were on the swinging door through which Cecilio had gone. Anger burned in me at their treasonous sisterhood.

"What's with the busboy?" Frank asked.

"It's the aerobics guy," Denise said.

"I guess this is his secret life," Frank replied with a snort.

"It's probably just a sideline to his Amway distributorship," I said feeling the rush an embezzler must experience after a close call. I wondered if Anthea felt the same excitement.

I began to look forward to my workouts with Cecilio. I watched the clock as the afternoons waned and the light shifted on the papers lying on my desk. The stark world of the weight room reached out to me through the final, stagnant hour of the workday. I developed a craving for the sharp overhead lighting that revealed the lines around my mouth and eyes and the thickness of my waist. I had come to like the simplicity of the chromed-steel curl bars and black-upholstered benches.

Cecilio barely said anything during our training sessions except to count out in his soft voice the number of repetitions as I did pull-downs or seated rows. In my fourth and fifth sets of bicep curls, he would sometimes reach out with one or two fingers of his hand and softly nudge my elbow back into position at my side as I strained to bring the bar through the final range of motion. There were times when I wondered if he guided Anthea's face and lips to his own in the same tender way.

Sometimes I imagined Anthea taking him back to the same place and time where she and I had fallen in love, to the hidden country where all women take their lovers. I saw her reading Neruda and Akhmatova to him as she had once read them to me. In my mind, I watched her pour the fire of her eyes and her voice into him until his insides glowed. In those moments, I could not have said whether I hated Anthea because she had chosen Cecilio, a dishwasher and a busboy, over me, or if I hated myself because I could no longer inspire such passion in her.

One warm July evening, after my workout with Cecilio, I walked out of the Y and went west on Burgundy Street, which gleamed like a thick steel rail under the sun's departing fire. I felt the tightness in my arms as blood raced to revive the muscles. The bands of my chest muscles breathed with a million tiny mouths and I felt every molecule of the cool air on the skin of my face. In that moment, I forgot about the office, Anthea, and Cecilio. I felt only the rhythm of my legs and the soft rush of air going in and out of my lungs. I imagined that, if I ran fast enough, I could overtake the sun and bathe in its yellow, cleansing light.

One night, as Anthea and I sat on opposite ends of the couch watching a TV sitcom, she asked, "Are you seeing someone else?"

I looked up at her and, for an instant, I was inside of her pale blue eyes looking back at myself, picturing me alone in the office with a twenty-six-year-old receptionist or a forty-two-year-old recently divorced accounts manager. And then I slid back into myself, seeing her over coffee with Cecilio, looking into his brown eyes. I saw her sitting in bed with him after their lovemaking, the smell of him fresh on her skin. I inhaled deeply, filling the reservoir of my lungs the way that I did in the weight room just before starting an exercise. "You've got a lot of nerve."

"It's just that you've been spending a lot of hours after work at the office. When you're here, you seem somewhere else."

"I've been preoccupied with work, the same things that I've been centered on for the last fourteen years in case you might not have noticed." I took a breath. "Besides, I could say the same about you."

"You haven't given me an answer."

For a moment I stared at her, imagining myself saying yes, conjuring up a woman's name, a face, a job description, and the female version of Cecilio. All that it would take was a soft nod of my head and she could go to hell with that son-of-a-bitch Cecilio. "No. I'm not seeing anyone." I said, letting my voice rise. And then I asked, "What about you? Anybody new in your life?"

I watched her mouth harden itself into a straight, thin line. Then she rose and left the room.

Go ahead and run, but I've got your number, I thought.

"Don't forget to smile," said Cecilio as I finished the last rep of my fifth set of decline presses. It was the first full sentence I'd heard from him in weeks. I set the bar onto the rack and heard the plates clang just before I broke down laughing. Slowly, I sat up. "The weight-meister speaks," I said. "I'll buy you dinner and a drink if you think you can manage at least ten complete sentences."

He slid one of the plates onto the weight tree and said, "Yeah, okay. But I've got to get back here. I want to get a workout in before my Spanish class."

"You know Shad's?" I said, picking a restaurant on the other end of the spectrum from Don Juanito's.

"Used to work there."

"I'll give you a ride."

"You go ahead. It's only a quarter-mile. I'll meet you there in twenty-minutes."

Shad's was a small, booth-and-counter restaurant in a neighborhood of run-down apartments, used car lots, and auto parts stores. It was the only place in town that had grits and eggs on the breakfast menu. You didn't go there if you were looking for a latte. The waitress was a middle-aged woman with a hard face and a burn scar on her right arm. Nothing on the plastic covered menu cost more than five dollars and fifty cents. Cecilio walked in, carrying a big, black gym bag. He was wearing green sweats and a pair of immaculate running shoes. He put a hardbound intermediate Spanish textbook on the table and sat down.

"Want a beer?" I asked.

"*Agua, solamente,*" he replied, opening a square plastic box containing a lot of tablets, some of which must have been a half an inch in diameter. "Protein tabs, vitamin C, multivitamins, and rutin," he replied to my unspoken question.

"Won't those things hurt on an empty stomach?"

"That's what the protein caps are for."

"Aren't you going to have anything else? It's on me," I said, thinking that he might be short on money.

"No thanks. I don't eat. I mean at restaurants."

This was starting out very weirdly, I thought. Was he one of those food conspiracy theorists, a precious-bodily-fluid freak right out of Doctor Strangelove? Maybe my wife thought his craziness was refreshing.

"Are you on a specialized diet?" I asked.

He swallowed one of the large tablets and chased it with a big swallow of water. "I'm on a special workout routine. I have to watch what I eat." He popped another tablet into his mouth and took another swallow of water. "Have to get the most out of what I take in."

"Must be some workout."

"Keeps me jumping."

"How many times a day do you work out?"

"Weights, twice a day. Sometimes three times a day when I can make the time."

"I hear you do aerobics, too."

"Twice a day."

"How do you keep from falling over at work? I mean, don't you get exhausted?"

He put two capsules filled with a pale green something into his mouth and swallowed the last of the water in his glass. "Not with this stuff."

A week later, I got Cecilio to meet me at Wolfgang's. The place was filled with the aromas of espresso, fresh-baked croissants, and bread. Cecilio pushed through the glass doors. He walked across the floor with a lighter, quicker stride than I'd seen him use that day at the restaurant where he worked. It was a stride that reminded me of my teens, of that beautiful energy that came of knowing that something wonderful is waiting just beyond the turn in the street or at the edge of the next minute. He sat down and smiled at me from across the table, looking at me through the steam coming off my coffee mug. Cecilio's black workout bag rested on the floor beside his chair, a shapeless, patient animal waiting for a word from him.

"Don't you ever get hungry being around all of that food?" I asked.

"I do. But I just take one of my protein drinks and some brewer's yeast. It goes away."

"How long have you been doing this?"

Cecilio's face tensed for a moment, crinkling the corner of his eyes, as though he was trying to push himself back through the current of time. He was so silent I thought he'd zoned out on me. I was about to repeat my question when he said, "Three years, twenty-nine months, and two weeks."

"What do you do when you're not working or in the gym?"

"Sleep," he replied. We both laughed.

"How did you get into this whole thing?"

"I did it so I could sleep. I didn't start off with the whole routine. You know, just some weight training. The running came next, then aerobics. I started doubling up on everything. I got tired."

"No shit!"

"The guy who runs the health food store told me that I was feeding on myself. Eating up muscle. He sold me a big can of protein drink powder. The less I ate, the better I felt."

"And sleep?"

"Incredible."

"Incredible?"

Cecilio stared at me for a moment and his brown eyes became focused and watchful, the way they had at our first meeting. Then he said, "I'm going to tell you something that's going to sound screwy." My stomach tightened, readying itself to accept this new fragment of him.

"When I was twenty-six, I had it all: Apartment, leather couch, and a badass car. Eight-hundred-dollar suits and sixty-five-dollar ties. I don't even want to tell you what I paid for my shoes. I had a girlfriend who turned heads from three blocks away." Cecilio sighed. "Emily," he said, opening the palms of his dark hands, upward and smiling, as though he was releasing a captive bird. "I was the hottest sales rep in men's clothing at Nordy's. I was on the management track, Jack." He picked up the eight-sided water glass, took a swallow of water and put the glass down softly.

I sat silently, looking into Cecilio's faraway eyes and trying to keep the image of him separate from Anthea.

"One night, I was driving Emily back to her place from a party. It was late and the streets were practically empty. I remember looking over at her, at the way the wind from the open window was blowing her hair back. And then there was nothing."

"Nothing?"

"I woke up two days later in a hospital bed with lots of bandages where the left side of my head should have been. They told me I'd run a red light and been hit by another car. Then they told me Emily was dead. I owed the hospital fifty-seven-thousand-dollars and I'd lost my driver's license because my car insurance went out of date three days before the accident." Cecilio tapped the left side of his head. "I walked out of the hospital two weeks later with this dent in my head and a hole where my life should have been. I stood on the sidewalk and for the first time in my life I understood how phony everything was: the trees, the buildings, even the sidewalk under my pricey shoes. I heard the sky and the sun laughing at me. I could've smashed the world to pieces just the way that lump-of-shit car from nowhere bent my face and wiped out my life." Cecilio paused and his mouth resolved itself into a hard line. Perhaps he tasted the memory of his rage.

I tried to imagine myself in Cecilio's place, Anthea dead, everything ruined, but I couldn't.

"I just lost it," he said. "I walked away from my job and my apartment. I took one change of clothes and got a room at the Y."

"And you started working out."

"At nights at first. It was the only thing that kept me from going crazy."

I thought about how the nearly empty weight room—with its floor covered with black rubber padding, its racks of black iron weight plates and its bars of chromed steel—would freeze out the past. Cecilio had entered a dark garden that would never bloom. I imagined him training with the desperation of a man who had nowhere else to go.

"I lost twenty-seven pounds in six weeks. My face was as sharp as a broken bottle. I lost so much fat that I looked like I'd been skinned." Cecilio laughed and the sound of his mirth was that of the wind going through dead grass. "The veins in my arms and chest looked like blue snakes. I didn't need anything, not even to eat," he said, his eyes shining with the memory of it. "I became someone else, a completely different guy," he said, giving me a don't-you-get-it smile.

"But you couldn't do that forever," I said.

He laughed. "I passed out in the middle of a step-aerobics class one day. One moment, I was jumping to the music and then I fell off that step like a shot bird. That night, the dreams started."

"What?"

"Like nothing I ever knew." Cecilio put a large round Vitamin C tablet into his mouth and chewed it. He took a swallow of water, leaned back into his chair, and told me he'd flown through the darkness of sleep to an old town lying on the green hip of a tropical, forested mountain. The air in the winding streets was

Geronimo G. Jagatac

warm and moist and the faded blue, pink, and rust-colored buildings had balconies with wrought iron railings. The dark-haired, dark-eyed people who filled the streets and the cafés looked into Cecilio's eyes, smiled and said, *"Buenos dias,"* as though they had known him since childhood. Cecilio looked past me, at what might have been the memory of that place, and said, "There was a place with an arched doorway and arched windows. Over the door hung a sign: Café Luna Verde. I could smell the aromas of *frijoles* and *chile verde*," he said. "And do you know something? For the first time in a whole year I was hungry."

We met at Wolfgang's the following Saturday. It was early in the morning and, from where I sat, I could see backlit clouds towering over the tops of the downtown buildings. Their edges were on fire. Cecilio came dressed in black sweats. The angles of his cheekbones had grown more prominent.

"You don't look well," I said.

"Thanks. And may you age quickly."

I laughed. "I was up late. What's your excuse?"

"I've lost a little weight. It's nothing. A few pounds up or down really shows on me."

"How the hell do you keep any muscle on you?"

"No esta importante, amigo," Cecilio said, shrugging.

"That city that you dream about. What's its name?" I asked, not trusting my Spanish enough to be able to ask the question.

He scrunched his face, deepening the shadow on his left side. *"Ay, yo no se! Pero es un ciudad muy amable."*

"They speak Spanish there, nothing else."

He nodded.

"You understand what they say, you talk to them?"

"Si, como no?"

"This is why you've been studying Spanish."

"Exactamente, Victorio," he replied, smiling at me the way a teacher might smile at a child who has solved a difficult problem.

"Cecilio, this is seriously strange," I said.

"Qué?" he replied, widening his eyes.

We broke into high, stuttering laughter, turning every head in Wolfgang's. But deep inside of me, I felt sadness because I realized now that Cecilio never wanted to be anything but a dishwasher with a buffed body or an extra shovel on a landscaping crew. He could have done anything he wanted to do, but he'd stripped everything from his life except his ability to dream.

With my heart pounding, I asked, "Do you know a woman named Anthea?"

He thought for a moment and said, "No, I don't think so. Who is she?"

"My wife. She's in your noon aerobics class."

Cecilio looked at me, shook his head, and shrugged his broad shoulders.

"She's a slim woman with black hair that reaches her shoulders. About half-an-inch taller than me."

He shook his head again.

Cecilio didn't show up for our next workout. Maybe he'd lied to me about not knowing Anthea. I worked out alone. I pictured Anthea and Cecilio loading up one of our cars with her sexiest outfits. She'd make sure to take a full checkbook and a wallet full of credit cards. Cecilio would throw his black workout bag onto the car's back seat and climb into the passenger's seat. They'd roll out of our driveway and down the street on their way to some big city or a mountain resort town. And I would take Cecilio's place in the weight room. A new life for all of us.

On my way out of the Y on the third night of my solitary workouts, I asked the woman at the front desk about Cecilio.

"I guess you didn't hear," she said. "He died in his room two nights ago. We didn't find him until yesterday morning."

"Wait a minute. Are you talking about Cecilio Santos?"

She nodded.

"Christ!"

There was a long pause and then she said, "He wasn't eating and he was doing these heavy workouts. Heart attack." She shook her head softly. "Do you know what we found in his apartment?" When I just stared at her, she said, "Eight sets of sweats, three pairs of workout shoes, and one set of street clothes. The place was full of vitamins and protein powders. Just bottles and jars of that stuff in his cabinets. You know what they found in his fridge? Half-a-head of cauliflower. I'm surprised he didn't die on you in the weight room."

My insides numbed. I turned and walked away.

She called after me, "He could have been on steroids. That could have kicked him over the edge."

I knew better.

Early the next afternoon, I went to the weight room where Cecilio and I had spent so many hours. I walked alone among the workstations and I felt the same

Geronimo G. Tagatac   79

emptiness in my chest that Cecilio must have felt walking out of the hospital. I sensed the same falseness in the walls and the light.

When I left the gym, the sun was flaring on the western edge of the city, turning the horizon into the edge of a badly chipped knife blade. I would go home and look into my wife's face. I told myself that I would try again to see in her eyes the woman I'd fallen in love with years ago. Maybe it was too late because that younger, fiery woman was lost to me the way Cecilio's lover had been taken from him that night at that intersection.

I walked down the street with my workout bag swinging at my side and I thought about Cecilio's spare, comfortless life. Had I or anyone else meant anything to him in the light of that city where the morning air was warm and everywhere he went he saw familiar faces? I imagined him walking along winding streets where the air bore the smells of *frijoles*, fried eggs, and warm corn tortillas. I pictured him entering the Café Luna Verde and speaking to the waitress, who smiled at his stilted Spanish. At last, I thought, Cecilio could sit down and eat his fill.

And I will tell you a story

by Nancy Flynn

how the tree grew out of the piano
how the piano came to float
upright
out of the house on Anthracite Ave.
during those three days in June
our Agnes Flood splintered the door
wide-freeing the black, the white
keys from their silent, undone
sostenuto extending down the street

how the piano came to the traffic light
corner of Center & Main
how it crossed, made it as far as
the dike where it struck, lifted then lodged
into that bank of earth
the one that had failed at its first
duty to keep the necessary river out

how the piano stayed
unnoticed by the dump trucks bridging the borough
those weeks after
the waters receded & everything by then was
mud & dust & rust & reek & piles
of the ruined & disheveled
a dissonance from every curb
prolonged

how the piano remained
(seemingly) sight unseen
how silt from the spring thaw pressed in
rush & deposit
made a window box of its hammers & strings

how an accidental samara—maple or ash?—
settled, split, grew a green
sprout in one year
tremelo stick in two
a sapling by five that would have taken
stronger arms than Samson's to root out

how the tree grew & grew & grew
how a lonely woman one day walking
weeding the dike of trash
came upon it marooned,
parted the foliage, scooped
her fingers into the damp
once hornbeam chords now crumbling
compost from felt

noted it was a piano
noted it accompanied a tree

carried a ladder from her home on the Flats
to lean against
to climb inside its quiet
études, serenades
climbed into the honky-tonk, topmost branch
where she saw

yet again
for the first time
yet again
time & again
the river that remained

pedaling horizontal
over-strung & tonic
loud/blood
artery & vein

one more world
between
the sharp, the flat

Easter

by Patrick Mathiasen

66You're so handsome, honey. You're so handsome!"

My mother sits in her wheelchair, leaning forward and smiling. Her grin reaches out toward me, surrounding me like a warm hand.

"You're just beautiful. Just perfect. But do you feel all right, honey? Is everyone okay?"

I wrap my fingers around her hand. Her fingers are long and thin and cold, and they stop trembling when I squeeze them.

"I'm fine, Mom. Everyone's fine."

She frowns.

"You're so handsome, honey. You're beautiful. Just perfect. But is everyone all right? Is Mikey all right?"

"I am Michael," I say. "I'm your son, Mom."

I squeeze her hand again, a couple of times, and then I reach out with my other hand to touch her, patting her on the arm. I can feel the thin skin beneath her synthetic blouse and the bony forearm under the skin.

She looks at me and frowns.

"You're not Michael. No, you're not. I know you're not," she says.

My mother begins to look up and down the hallway, and she pulls away from me. Her hands drop to her sides and then the screams come as they have with each visit I have made over the past few months.

"Help! Help! Help me! *Help me! Help!*"

I know what's coming, and I try to head it off.

"It's okay. Everything's okay. There's nothing to— "

But I'm too late. The fear leaps into her eyes like an animal trapped, and the sound of her screams echo up and down the narrow hallway of the nursing home where she lives.

"Help, help, help! Get him away from me. He doesn't live here. He looks like Michael, but he's not Michael. He's trying to trick me."

My mother spins around in her wheelchair until she faces me. "You dirty bastard, you won't get away with it," she says.

In the hallway, all of the visitors on this Easter Sunday are looking at me now. I straighten up and take two steps back, away from my mother's wheelchair. I wish I could disappear, but there's no escape. An aide appears at my side.

"Helen, Helen, it's all right," she says. "There's nothing to worry about. This is your son, Michael, and he brought you some chocolate. You like chocolate, don't you?"

The aide, Jamaica, pushes a piece of See's Candy toward my mother's mouth.

"It's all right," I say to the aide. "I think it's just been too much for her today with all of the people visiting and everything."

Jamaica smiles. My mother is trying to push the chocolate truffle into her ear. It breaks open, and the liquid inside runs down the side of her face and out over her multicolored blouse.

"Goddammit!" she says. "Now look what I've done."

My mother runs her hands over the dissolving candy, trying to brush it away. Her hands become covered with the brown, sticky substance, and it covers the front of her blouse in long streaks. Her shriek pierces the air again.

It takes a long time to calm my mother down and even longer to clean the chocolate and to change her clothes. While the aides do this, I walk down the hall and out the front door into the bright, cold Midwestern day. It's a relief to get away from my mother for a few minutes, and I take a deep breath and light a cigarette out in the parking lot.

It didn't start like this. Not at all. It started with small lapses in memory, forgetfulness when she would neglect to return phone calls or not show up for lunch dates. But it was ominous, even at first, and I remember it now.

My mother, with her love for doing crossword puzzles, gradually stopped doing the puzzles. My mother, who loved to read biographies of great men, slowly stopped reading books. I didn't notice at first. I lived way out on the West Coast, and she lived in the Midwest. But soon, the phone calls began to come, from my brother and then my niece, telling me there was something wrong.

I was the expert, the psychiatrist, the doctor in the family whom the others all turned to for advice. What was wrong? That was the question. What was going wrong with your mother, Michael?

I took time off from my work, at first a few days, then more and more until it was weeks at a time as I located a neurologist near my mother's small home-town—Sauk Rapids, Minnesota—and took her back and forth for the visits, and the blood tests, and the brain scans. She hated all of it, of course, and she let me know it every time I came to pick her up.

It wasn't just my work that I left behind but all of my life, my wife and our

Patrick Mathiasen

friends, our weekends together reading the papers and talking and going out to movies and doing all of those things that couples do together. And so my resentment toward my mother began to build as I flew back and forth to see her. Soon, the pieces of my life began to mix together as if pushed into a small tight space, a bag with no air to breathe.

"You want to put me in one of those places, don't you?" my mother said.

Each time I saw her, she shouted the question and stared at me, her eyes dark and heavy. She meant a nursing home, but she couldn't think of the name for the place. She didn't believe that I was trying to help her. That anyone wanted to help her. As her memory failed, more and more, she retreated down further and further into the hidden cave of her paranoia to a place where I could not reach her, could not touch her.

Alzheimer's Disease. Those were the words of the young neurologist after the testing, scans, and memory tests were completed. I knew it long before he said it, but it didn't help being the family "expert" who had spent much of his life working around the edges of this thief of memory. It was more painful, in fact, to have this happen to my mother after having seen the ravages of this disease in my own patients over the years: I thought I knew what was coming.

I finally had to move back to this little town in the Midwest, to this place that I had spent my life trying to escape. There was no one else to help her—she had alienated everyone else with her anger and cruelty. My brother no longer spoke to her. His children, her grandchildren, were afraid of her rage and hatred.

So this left me alone with my mother. My wife was the one who suggested that we move.

"You have to do it," she said. "You'll hate yourself if you don't."

And so I closed my practice in Seattle. I found work near this tiny town in the Midwest, and we moved across the country. But I resented it. I resented it deeply.

Out across the way, in the parking lot of the nursing home, I see a family crawling out of their blue Subaru wagon. A mom, a dad, and two little girls—maybe six or seven years old—twins dressed in bright Easter colors like painted eggs.

Out here in the parking lot, I had almost forgotten it was Easter. I inhaled the smoke from my cigarette and tapped the end with my index finger. The ashes drifted down and blew away in the wind.

Easter. I remember my family—my parents, and my brother, and me—coming together in the backyard of our home here in Sauk Rapids. We would watch the big golden Labrador—my brother's dog, King—run through the grass with his nose to the ground, sniffing out the Easter eggs that had been buried all over the backyard and pawing at them until they sprung up and out from their hiding places.

It was my parent's ritual, this hiding of the eggs on Easter. This is what Easter meant to us. And it brought on peals of laughter as the dog found one after another of the painted Easter eggs and his jaws closed down around them and the yellow yolks splayed out over the green grass in our backyard.

I remembered my mother watching and screaming at the dog in her high-pitched voice. "Stop that, King. Stop it. Goddamn you. Goddamn dog."

I remembered her picking up rocks and throwing them at the dog, always missing him, and then screaming at my brother, Joseph.

"Make him stop, Butch. Make that damn dog of yours stop that shit."

That's what she called my brother—his nickname, Butch. She called him that throughout his life. My brother and I would laugh, harder and harder, and the angrier my mother became, the harder we would laugh as the yolk of the eggs sprayed all over the yard and the tiny flecks of colored shells exploded from the dog's mouth.

As I thought of it now, it seemed as if the dog was getting one over on my mother. He was winning. He was doing something neither my brother nor I could ever do.

The little girls are fighting with each other now, in the parking lot of the nursing home, and one pulls at the other's hair as their parents look on with exhausted expressions. Then the dad moves forward and takes hold of the arm of one of his daughters, the one pulling at the other's hair, and jerks her away. I can hear his loud voice from across the parking lot.

"I told you to stop that, Miriam. Now stop it!"

The words come out of his mouth in a hiss into the cold bright air.

"Owww! Owww! Stop that. It hurts. You're hurting me!" the little girl cries out.

Their mom looks as if she would rather be just about anywhere but where she is. She sees me watching, and she leans forward and nudges her husband and whispers something to him. He straightens and lets go of his little girl's arm, and the group starts to quickly walk across the parking lot. They pass under the arc and into the nursing home.

Patrick Mathiasen

I take one more deep drag on my cigarette and flip it down onto the pavement as I start to walk back toward the nursing home, following along behind the two little girls and their parents. As I pass inside the door, the warmth hits me. The moans and screams rise up with the warm air and the odors, and I see the aging faces of many of the people who live here. I try to hold my breath as I walk down the hallway, but I can't for very long. I decide to stop to use the restroom before heading back to my mother's room.

When I come out, I see my mother sitting in the dining room in her wheelchair, wearing a flannel nightgown that I bought for her many years ago. All of the chocolate has been cleaned off her face. She is surrounded by several of the nursing home staff.

Surrounded by staff? Why is she surrounded by all of these people?

Jamaica sees me and takes hold of my arm.

"You're here, Mr. Michael. You're here," she says. "Come see what she's done!"

Jamaica takes hold of my hand and pulls me forward, and my feet move in short choppy steps toward the crowd of people in the middle of the dining room.

Someone is crying. At first I think it's my mother. But it's not. Her face pops into view, and she is scowling. Her fists are raised and balled up tightly, and she is saying something. Her mouth moves, but I can't make out the words.

On the floor in front of my mother, a small form lies facedown. As I get closer, I can see that it's a child. It's one of the little girls that I saw in the parking lot in her Easter-egg dress. Next to her head, a spot of red is seeping out, spreading onto the white carpet. The little girl is not moving. She is lying still on the ground, and the crowd of people that surround her look on.

"Don't move her," someone says. "Leave her alone until the medical folks get here. She might be hurt."

As I get closer to the small form on the ground, it looks as if the girl is frozen, glued to the floor. The girl's sister stands next to her, looking down at her with a bored expression. And behind both of them, the child's mother sits on the ground with her hand on her injured daughter's back. It is she who is crying, sending a shrill wailing sound out over the heads of the people gathered around her.

My mother's words rise up into the air—faint at first, then louder and louder. "You bastard! You dirty little bastard!" she says.

My mother's lips curl back, revealing her yellowed teeth, as she repeats the words over and over—"bastard, bastard, bastard, bastard"—until the words ring out like a mantra into the warm nursing home air.

The little girl—her name was Becky—was okay. An ambulance came and took her to the hospital and she was X-rayed and examined and hospitalized for a few days, and she survived with a fractured right cheekbone. I went to visit her, to try to explain to her what had happened. But all she could say to me was, "Why did that mean woman hit me? I didn't do anything to her."

I knew exactly how she felt. On the day that this happened, the nursing home staff informed me that my mother could no longer live there. It was not safe to have her around any of their residents. I would need to find another place for her to live.

And so I began the long, maybe impossible process of finding a place where my mother could live out the rest of her days. My wife thought that she should live with us, that we should set up a room in our new home for her, and that we bring her into our house.

My wife, Monica, was a saint. The thought of living under the same roof with my mother frightened me—a fear that seeped into me, down through me like pain spreading out in circles through my body, wider and wider until it covered me like cold water.

I couldn't do it. I knew that I couldn't, and so I began a search for another nursing home that would provide a place for my mother to live out her life. But it was the same answer, over and over. The same damn answer. *We would love to take your mother in, sir, but with her ... the unfortunate times when she becomes agitated, well, we just don't have the staff that can handle that kind of thing. Sir.*

Always the sir punctuating their sentences, the awkward, contorted sign of respect when they really mean your *mother is a dangerous, wild woman—an animal we can't contain in our pleasant little place.* Always the same, in these places with names like "Pleasant Arms" and "Sunset Palms," and on and on and on.

The resentment climbed up through my thoughts, higher and higher until it covered me like a prickly wool blanket that pulled the sweat out of me in a cold, shivering drenching of water.

My wife and I moved her in with us, into a room upstairs in our house that had served as my office, the place where I tried to write poetry when I had the

Patrick Mathiasen

time. Poetry. Now it was gone, replaced by this sad, heaving woman whose thoughts had slowly mixed together in her mind, until they made little sense at all.

We kept looking for a place for her, of course. I kept calling nursing homes, bundling my mother up in our car, and driving her to this or that place for visits. But none would take her in. The last one we tried was a place called "Home, Sweet Home."

It was out in the country, maybe five miles from Sauk Rapids. I remembered rolling my mother into the office of the director of the nursing home. He was a large, tanned man wearing an ill-fitting blue suit with a red tie that hung just a little too far down below his belt. He started talking right away, even before we had a chance to settle into the space in front of his desk.

"We don't like to think of ourselves as a nursing home," he said. "No, no, no. Not at all."

He shook his right index finger back and forth in the air as he said this, to make his point. I watched it flash back and forth, the bronze flesh on his wrist jiggling up and down below his hand. My mother watched it, too, and a frown appeared on her face as he went on.

"We think of our place as a true home, an environment where our staff can hold your loved ones in their arms, much as you would hold them in your own home—*if* only you could."

He emphasized the word *if*, almost spitting it out into the air as he looked down at my mother in her wheelchair. Then he bent over her, reached out with his hand, and put it on her shoulder. He leaned in close to her face and smiled.

"We try to think of you as part of our family when you live here," he said.

These were the last words he said to my mother. Her frown deepened, and her right hand gripped his red tie. Then she pushed back in her wheelchair, grabbing at the tie with her left hand as well. The tie pulled tight around the man's neck. It all happened so fast.

As I leapt to my feet and took hold of my mother's hands, the veins in the man's face and neck popped out, dark blue against the tan of his skin. I tried to pull my mother's hands free from his tie, but she wouldn't let go.

The man gasped, and his mouth opened wide—but no words came out. Only a long, strained gasp that blew through the room as he fell to his knees in front of my mother's wheelchair.

I kept trying to loosen my mother's grip from the tie, and, finally, she let go. The man's hands went up to his neck, and he fastened them onto the tie, pulling at it until it came loose from his throat and he could breathe. Still on the floor, his chest heaved as he waved his arms back and forth like a man drowning.

That was the last nursing home I took my mother to visit. It became clear at that point—very clear—that my mother would live with us in our home for the rest of her life.

The rest of her life. How long would that be? I had no idea. She was in good health. As her memory faded, her physical strength seemed to improve, and she became stronger and stronger. It could be five years, ten years, or even more that I would hear her shuddering, strained breathing passing over her lips behind the closed door of my former office, waking me in the early morning hours each of my days.

We hired caregivers, of course, two women who could be there for twelve hours a day to help take care of her. These two women would come in around eight in the morning to get my mother up out of bed. They would wash her, feed her, and spend time talking to her. But they were gone by late in the evening, and Monica and I would be left to deal with her through the rest of the night.

My life changed in ways I could never have imagined after my mother moved in to our home with us. She became a constant presence in my thoughts during my days at work, pressing up into the curves and synapses of my brain, spreading out against the inside of my skull harder and harder until my vision blurred when I tried to listen to what my patients were trying to tell me about their own lives. I found it hard to concentrate, hard to focus on my work. I started to forget things about my patients; I started to miss details that were important to their treatment.

In the evenings, on my way home from work, I began to dread my arrival in my driveway. I had always enjoyed sitting down with Monica at the end of a day, to have coffee and talk about the more interesting patients that I had seen. But not anymore. Now I would sit down with anxiety and ask if my mother had done anything dreadful. Had she hit one of her caregivers? Had she broken anything? These were the questions I now asked my wife.

Poetry had been an outlet for me, a way to make sense of my work and my life. I had been writing since I finished my residency training in psychiatry. It had been one of my dreams to publish a book of poetry. Now this was gone— vanished as my mother's heaving body moved into what had been my office sanctuary where I once wrote my poems. She covered everything with her shudders and her white, damp flesh until I could think of nothing else but her when I entered the room. This was one of the hardest things about it all. The loss of a dream of something exciting and exhilarating.

I could not tell if my mother wanted to stay with us in our home. Most of the time, she didn't recognize my wife or me. She would eat when food was placed in front of her, and she would sit and watch TV with us in her room. But the only thing that seemed to remain, the only thing of who she had been, was her anger. When she spoke, which was rare, the words that came out were sharp-edged, like pieces of glass. Words like *dirty, hate, stupid, bastard,* and on and on, words repeated over and over until they had no meaning like empty threats.

About six months after my mother had moved in with us, I came home from work and I found Monica sitting at the kitchen table with her head bent down over her arms. She was sobbing, and the sound spread out through the room.

I was alarmed. My wife almost never cried.

"What's the matter, Monica?" I asked.

No answer. I bent down and put my hand on her shoulder. This time, I shook her arm back and forth as I asked her again.

"What happened, babe?"

She turned her face up toward me, her eyes red.

"You don't want to know," she said.

Monica's head fell back on the table, and the slow, racking sobs returned.

I knew it was something my mother had done. I sat down at the table, across from my wife, and I waited for her to tell me what had happened.

What seemed like a long time passed, and then Monica sat up and looked at me. She wiped her sleeve across her eyes, brushing the tears away. Then she smiled a weak smile and reached her hand out to take mine. I looked into my wife's eyes, and I thought again of how beautiful she was.

"I can't stay here any longer, Michael," she said. "Not while your mother lives here."

I tried to speak, but Monica cut me off. She raised her finger to her lips, to quiet me, and then she spoke again.

"It's not you. It's not your fault. She is … "

She struggled for the words.

"She's evil."

I didn't know what to say. I stared at my wife.

"What did she say to you, Monica? What did she say?"

The question hung in the air between us at the kitchen table. Then Monica told me what had happened.

"Michael, she was clear in her thoughts, completely lucid. I couldn't believe it. She had been talking to me most of the day. And then we were watching television, an old show about a talking horse."

"Mr. Ed?" I asked.

"Yes. Yes, that's the one. And she looks up at me, and she says, 'God didn't want you to—'"

Monica starts crying again, and she can't finish. I grip her hand tighter. She squeezes back, and finally she gets it out.

"She said God didn't want me to have Bobby. That I didn't deserve a child."

"Oh, God," I said.

Bobby was the only child Monica and I had been able to conceive. He had died in his sleep as a baby, many years ago, at the age of six months. My wife had never really recovered from the loss. She had never been able to move on.

The thought of Monica moving out of our home, of leaving me, was too much. I couldn't let it happen. She had become the only thing in my life that I felt I could hold on to, as my mother moved into and through my home like the wind, gaining speed and blowing everything in its path aside.

I begged Monica to stay. I told her I would find a place for my mother, away from our home.

"But we've tried that, Michael. We've tried everything," she said.

It was true. I had gone to every setting that I could think of, every nursing home and assisted living place in our region, and none of them would take my mother. Not a one.

"Then we can try something else, Monica. You can't just leave. Please don't. I can get twenty-four hour caregivers for her so you don't ever have to do anything for my mother again. You won't even need to see her. We can just have the caregivers deal with her, take her food and clean her, and leave her up on the second floor—out of sight."

For a moment, I thought this might work. Until I looked into my wife's eyes, until I saw their blue-gray color deepen and harden around the black pupils, like stone around deep still water.

"Michael, it just won't work. You know it won't work. She would still be here in our house, a breathing, living thing, a reminder for me of the pain of losing my baby."

Monica looked away from me, and she began to cry again. It was then that I knew there was nothing I could do. Through her tears, my wife spoke in a low, soft voice.

"I love you, Michael. You know I do. But I just can't stay here. It's not forever, my leaving, you know. It's just until … " She paused. And then she finished her sentence. "Until she's gone."

Monica moved out of our home, just as she said that she would. I thought of going with her. Of course I did. I thought of hiring people to watch and care for my mother twenty-four hours a day, of paying them enough to put up with my mother, and of just leaving her in my home and moving out with Monica.

But I couldn't do it. I wanted to, but I could not. Somehow my mother had become—no, had always been—more than the old woman lying in my office upstairs breathing in and out, the old woman who had brought her anger and hatred into my home. She was also … my mother. She had brought me into this world. She was a part of me, and I a part of her as well. Our genes were mixed together, in the long intertwined rope of DNA. As much as I wanted to, I could not separate myself from her presence.

After my wife left, after I hired more caregivers to help with my mother, I would sometimes walk up the steps to my mother's room at night. I would try to be as quiet as I could, creeping softly on my slippers, and I would peek around the corner and into her room. If my mother was asleep, I would watch her chest rise and fall, and I would remember times with her many years ago, back when I was a child.

It was then that I could see my mother singing religious hymns while she played with me and my new Irish Setter puppy, Rex, in the kitchen of my boyhood home, preparing a breakfast of French toast for all of us—me and her and the dog. That's what she did. She cooked a big breakfast for all of us. It was so different from my memories of Easter.

This new memory caused me to laugh and cry, all at the same time. I had to put my hand over my mouth, to quiet the sound, so that I did not wake my mother as I walked back down the steps of my house.

In My Home Village

by Penelope Scambly Schott

All night coyotes crooned around my bed.
This morning four school girls in hoodies

came to write poems at my kitchen table
and I was happy like an oak with acorns.

When the local fire siren sounded at noon,
horses down by the creek lifted their heads.

The afternoon was perfect. Our wet planet
kept rotating without my close supervision

while the cold North Pole and South Pole
called to each other through molten rock.

When "D" hill rolled east to block the sun,
clouds above the mountain throbbed pink.

Just now a rainbow trout swam me to bed
where the Dipper drips sleep on my eyes.

I think dying might feel like this – luscious
and complete, the tremble after the love.

Gari with Spicy Peanut Sauce, Peace Corps Gabon Style

by Anna Monders

Manioc (cassava) is a staple food in Central and West Africa. Dried manioc flakes, known as gari, *are cooked in water until they form a thick white substance that can be rolled into balls. The subtleness of the* gari *is a marvelous base for spicy peanut sauce.*

1. Take plastic yellow cup and four 100-franc coins—the ones with antelopes on one side—up the hill to friend Nimata's food stand. Sit on short stool made of coiled liana vines and visit for a while. Ask after her health, her family, her chickens.

2. Eventually, ask if there is any *pâte d'arachide*. Hold out yellow plastic cup while Nimata transfers two large spoonfuls of peanut butter into it. Teach friend how to say *peanut butter* since she would like to add English to the eight languages she already knows.

3. Watch Nimata fill clear plastic bags with dried manioc flakes. At her urging, decide *gari* and peanut sauce will make an excellent dinner. Buy small bag of *gari* and, for the cat, four smoked sardines wrapped in old paper.

4. Scratch arms where invisible but itchy midge-like *fou-rous* are biting skin. Give Nimata 400 francs, about 60 cents, for purchases. Say goodnight as she goes inside for prayer time.

5. Return home to cement brick house. Do not notice rusting metal roof, torn green mosquito netting, or uneven cement floor.

6. Retrieve old journal from under red cloth hammock strung between bedroom's window frame and doorframe. Discover journal is mildewing and binding is coming loose. Celebrate delights of a hot and humid January.

7. Open to inside back cover of journal and read handwritten peanut sauce

recipe: garlic, ginger, lemon juice, oil, soy sauce, chili powder, peanut butter, water. Let eyes linger on *soy sauce* and indulge in quiet moment of nostalgia.

8. Take fresh ginger out of pink plastic bowl on kitchen windowsill. Peel with large kitchen knife—oversized, but better than the machete. Fetch grater off hook where it hangs in the company of three pans and two palm-sized spiders named Bonnie and Clyde. Wash away cobwebs and acknowledge this will never be a *cheese* grater since the only so-called cheese available in the village is 55% fat Laughing Cow soft cheese spread. Grate ginger, using side of grater with small holes.

9. Chop clove of garlic. Remember grandmother's garlic press.

10. Add approximately one-half cup of previously boiled and filtered water to small saucepan. Light one of two burners on gas stovetop and let water begin to heat. Be thankful not to be cooking outside, balancing pan on three cement bricks and getting ash in food. Hope gas company does not go on strike again soon.

11. Add garlic, ginger, and oil to saucepan, along with remaining peanut butter that has not yet been nibbled away.

12. Find one last green—but ripe—lemon the size of a golf ball among garlic, onions, and old bread in plastic colander on kitchen shelf. Slice lemon in half, squeeze liquid into mug and strain seeds out with a fork. Add the juice to saucepan and throw peels and seeds out kitchen window for immediate composting.

13. Stir peanuty-lemony-garlicky-gingery concoction in saucepan until texture is smooth. Add pinch of salt from glass jar left behind by former house resident. Follow with dash of pepper from spice jar left behind by *former* former house resident. Finish off with cumin from jar sent from home, which always brings memories of guacamole. Remove newly minted peanut sauce from stovetop.

14. Put water on to boil for *gari*. Wash dishes at cold water spigot above black plastic tub, also known as "sink." Add manioc flakes to boiling water. Stir. Add more water. Mash lumps. Turn off fire.

Anna Monders 97

15. Unwrap dried fish for cat, throw heads and skin out back door, and mix fish meat and small portion of *gari* in a blue plastic bowl.

16. Roll remaining *gari* into three not-quite-fist-sized balls and place on plate. Cover with spicy peanut sauce.

17. Carry plate, chipped mug of water, and cat's blue plastic bowl of fishy *gari* out to living room. Set plates down on coffee table and floor, according to species of intended recipient.

18. Turn on fan, ignoring lack of front safety cover, and pick up *War and Peace* from yellow flowered cushion on wicker chair. Open book to page 953 of 1440. Sprawl in chair. *Bon appétit!*

Trestle

by Graham Murtaugh

We don't know from rage.

Only: post holes shoulder-wide
      fence wire unspooling down I-90
      drainage ditch running brown
      Skoal-stained lower lips

Shuck corn, beans; later: shirts
      at the slough, us boys with our daddy-hands
already swollen (slap-back rough
      -housing) girl-hips hitched up
watch us not watching. Mooning. Icehouse. Cigarettes
      stolen out the drawer. Stay up-river
of the sour eddy, jagged hole—

Dark shoal
      of tailings, snags, sunken junk
where brother Quinn came down
      a year ago, June, harvest-high,
one last late-night, tight-roping
      the trestle with Old Tom, tippling,

singing:

don't you know
a ditch's just a grave
with the ends kicked out?

Oh, don't you know
dirt measures our steps?

Midnight train came to right the balance.

Sad, sad Quinny, red-faced clown
face down

Don't mean to but do:
shake the jar of lightning bugs
so hard
the inside glows

Contributors

Faith Allington is a Washington resident originally from California. Her poems have recently appeared or are forthcoming in *Crab Creek Review*, *Floating Bridge Review*, *Cascadia Review* and *King County's Poetry on Buses*.

Richard Beckham II is the author of two novels, *Frog in the Pot* and *The Tale of Mu*, and has had stories published by *Metazan*, *Yesteryear Fiction*, and *Innovative Fiction Magazine*. He has an MFA from Antioch University Los Angeles and his blog can be found at www.richardbeckham.com.

Susan Blackaby is a Portland children's book author and winner of the 2011 Lion and the Unicorn Award for Excellence in North American Poetry. Dabbling across genres in children's literature is familiar ground; wandering beyond those boundaries is a relatively recent and uncharted adventure.

Les Brady's short fiction has appeared in *Reed Magazine* and *Blue Earth Review*. He holds an MFA in Creative Writing from San Jose State University. He teaches Creative Writing at the Art Institute of California—Silicon Valley. www.lesbrady.com

Harry Demarest has retired after vocations of scientific research, teaching, and working with computers, politics, and the Internet. He enjoys writing memoir, short stories, flash fiction, fifty-word stories, six-word stories, and children's stories. He lives in Corvallis, Oregon, where he likes to take care of grandchildren, play chess, and sleep.

Jay Duret is a San Francisco based writer and illustrator who blogs at www.jayduret.com. More than two-dozen of Jay's stories have been published or are forthcoming in online and print journals, including *Narrative Magazine*, *Blue Fifth Review*, *Gargoyle*, and *December*. Second Wind Publishing will publish Jay's first novel, *Nine Digits*, this year. More at www.ninedigits.com.

Nancy Flynn grew up on the Susquehanna River in northeastern Pennsylvania, spent many years on a downtown creek in Ithaca, New York, and now lives near the mighty Columbia in Portland. She attended Oberlin, Cornell, and has an M.A. from SUNY/Binghamton. Her most recent chapbook is *Eternity a Coal's Throw*. Her website is www.nancyflynn.com.

Patrick Mathiasen is a Psychiatrist, who lives and works in Seattle, Washington. He has published two non-fiction works in the past: *An Ocean of Time: Tales of Hope and Forgetting* (Scribner, 1997) and *Late Life Depression* (Dell, 1998). He has had a long-term interest in fiction, and writing short stories, and much of the material for his fiction arises from his clinical work. He is thrilled to have *Easter* published in *Gold Man Review*.

Elizabeth McLagan's poems have been published in journals including *Poetry Northwest*, *32 Poems*, *Beloit Poetry Journal*, *Zone 3*, and *Verse Daily*. Poems have won an AWP Intro award, the Frances Locke Memorial Award and the *Bellingham Review's* 49th Parallel Award. Her collection of poems *In The White Room* (CW Books) was published in 2013.

N.T. McQueen received his MA in Creative Writing from CSU-Sacramento and is the author of the novel, *Between Lions and Lambs*. He has won two Bazzanella Literary Awards and his work has appeared in *Transcendence*, *Burning Daylight*, and others. He lives in Northern California with his wife and three children.

Amy Miller's writing has appeared in *Gold Man Review*, *Rattle*, *Willow Springs*, and *ZYZZYVA*. A finalist for the Pablo Neruda Prize and 49th Parallel Award, she won the Cultural Center of Cape Cod National Poetry Competition, judged by Tony Hoagland. She lives in Ashland, Oregon, and blogs at writers-island. blogspot.com.

After college, Anna Monders joined the Peace Corps and served for two years as an environmental educator in Gabon, Africa. There, she indulged in fresh tropical fruit, reveled in equatorial rainstorms, and defied Peace Corps rules to work at a transition shelter for victims of child trafficking. Now she lives in Ashland, Oregon.

Graham Murtaugh, a third-generation Oregonian, lives and writes in the wilds of SE Portland. Outside his day job, he facilitates free writing workshops for incarcerated men and does his damndest to get lost in the woods. He recently published the illustrated chapbook *There Is No Safety*. See his work at graham-murtaugh.com

Liz Prato's stories and essays have appeared in numerous publications, including *Hayden's Ferry Review*, *The Rumpus*, *Iron Horse Literary Review*, *Subtropics*, and *ZYZZYVA*. She teaches, edits, and writes in Portland, Oregon. Her short story collection is forthcoming from Press 53 in May 2015, and she recently completed a memoir. www.lizprato.com

Penelope Scambly Schott has published several books including *A Is for Anne: Mistress Hutchinson Disturbs the Commonwealth*, which received an Oregon Book Award for Poetry. Her newest is *How I Became an Historian*. She lives in Portland and Dufur, Oregon where she teaches an annual poetry workshop.

Like everyone else, Kaz Sussman got into poetry because that's where the big bucks are. He is a carpenter, and lives in a home he has built in Oregon from abandoned poems. His work has appeared in *Caduceus*, *Raven Chronicles*, *Nimrod Journal*, *Stoneboat*, *Whitefish Review*, and *Gastronomica*. www.kazsussman.com

Geronimo G. Tagatac's short fiction has appeared in *Writers Forum*, *The Northwest Review*, *Alternatives Magazine*, *Orion Magazine*, *The Clackamas Literary Review*, *The Chautauqua Literary Review*, *Elohi Gadugi Journal*, and *Gold Man Review*. His first book of short fiction, *The Weight of the Sun*, was a 2007 Oregon Literary Arts finalist. Geronimo lives and writes in Salem, Oregon.

Joyce Tomlinson is a graduate of the MFA program in nonfiction writing at Pacific University in Forest Grove, Oregon. A lifelong resident of the Northwest, she now lives in Seattle, where she is at work on a full-length memoir.